S0-AZZ-005

ENOLA HOLMES

AND THE ELEGANT ESCAPADE

ENOLA HOLMES

AND THE ELEGANT ESCAPADE

Nancy Springer

WEDNESDAY BOOKS
NEW YORK

This is a work of fiction. All of the characters, organizations, and events portrayed in this novel are either products of the author's imagination or are used fictitiously.

First published in the United States by Wednesday Books, an imprint of St. Martin's Publishing Group

ENOLA HOLMES AND THE ELEGANT ESCAPADE. Copyright © 2022 by Nancy Springer. All rights reserved. Printed in the United States of America. For information, address St. Martin's Publishing Group, 120 Broadway, New York, NY 10271.

www.wednesdaybooks.com

Designed by Omar Chapa

The Library of Congress Cataloging-in-Publication Data is available upon request.

ISBN 978-1-250-82297-0 (hardcover)
ISBN 978-1-250-82298-7 (ebook)

Our books may be purchased in bulk for promotional, educational, or business use. Please contact your local bookseller or the Macmillan Corporate and Premium Sales Department at 1-800-221-7945, extension 5442, or by email at MacmillanSpecialMarkets@macmillan.com.

First Edition: 2022

10 9 8 7 6 5 4 3 2 1

To Jaime Fernando Pinto, with my love

ENOLA HOLMES

AND THE ELEGANT ESCAPADE

Prologue

Seventeen-year-old Lady Cecily Alistair took a knitting needle in her left fist and used its point quite forcibly to scratch a crude, life-sized caricature of her father on the inside of her locked bedroom door. Then she stepped back, barefoot, in her nightgown, to look at the pudgy, fat-headed portrait she had just etched in splintery brown scratches on the door's white paint. She could have done far better with paint or charcoal, but her father had not allowed her any when he had shut her in here a week ago. He had not allowed her journals to write in, either, or pencils, or pen, or books to read, or anything to do except knit, which he knew she did not like and never had, not even before.

Before it all happened, only a year ago, she had been an obedient if not particularly happy daughter, and all she had to worry about was preparing to be presented to the queen, practicing how to curtsey nearly to the floor without displacing the three large white feathers absurdly sprouting atop her coifed head. And, after that, "coming out" as a debutante and finding a suitably rich and titled husband.

Thinking about those times, Lady Cecily aimed her knitting needle like a dart and hurled it hard at the imaginary target of her father's heart—or lack of one.

Not that she had exactly *dreamed* of "coming out" or marriage, but she would have gone along with her parents' plans; it was not she who had spoilt them. Certainly, it was not her fault she had been hypnotized and *kidnapped*, of all things.

Lady Cecily's projectile clattered against the locked door but missed its target.

Frowning, picking it up to try again, she wondered not for the first time why she had been so meek, so docile, so utterly possessed by—by her family's expectations, yes, but more disturbingly, by the villain's power. He, the charismatic kidnapper, had Mesmerized her so that she might never have escaped his control if it were not for a strange, gawky, gallant girl named Enola who had appeared out of the night and, after rescuing Cecily and saving her life, disappeared back into the night as if she were a phantom.

Enola: mystery. Enola's name written backwards spelled "alone." If Cinderella had a fairy godmother, then Cecily seemed to have a fairly odd godsister.

If her life were a fairy tale, she would have returned home to live Happily Ever After, but not so. Papa had fulminated and thundered even though nothing had *happened* between his daughter and the kidnapper except that he had starved her, overworked her, and oh, by the way, tried to kill her. But to Papa, and most of society, this was all scandalous and she, Cecily, the victim, was soiled, stained, ruined matrimonial goods. She could never be presented at court, be a debutante, or attract an aristocratic husband.

Papa had not even given her time to recover from her ordeal before he had turned her over to his two odious sisters in a plot to have her marry, perforce, her toad-like cousin. Her darling father had very nearly succeeded in selling her like a slave into wedlock. She did manage, at a lucky chance encounter in a public lavatory, to slip a coded message to Enola, but with very little hope of rescue. By the morning of her nuptials, Cecily was so weakened by starvation and ill-usage that she would have let herself be dragged like a rag doll through the ceremony. She would have been shackled by law to a loathsome husband if it were not for Enola.

Enola, appearing at the last moment like a fairy-tale hero, or at least like a fairly tall one. Cecily had learned more about Enola that day, for Enola had delivered her to her brother, who had turned out to be the great detective Sherlock Holmes! So, Enola was Enola Holmes, but to Cecily it seemed as if . . . truly, somehow Enola was her very best friend even though they had only met twice, last January and last May . . . well, three times, if one included a very brief and wordless encounter in the First Ladies' Lavatory of London.

Sherlock Holmes had escorted Cecily to the safety of her mother's arms, and then, for a while, it had seemed as if all would be well. But far too soon, Papa had found them and taken them back, and he had imprisoned Cecily in her room, stating his intention to marry her off to someone, somehow, at the first opportunity. Not only had he deprived Cecily of her books and her art for punishment, but, to prevent even the most remote possibility of her escape, he had taken all of her clothes away.

Which was why, in the middle of a sunny October afternoon, she had nothing to wear except a nightgown and nothing better to do than scratch a big, fat likeness of her father on the inside of her locked bedroom door.

Cecily's hand, holding the knitting needle, tightened into a fist. And instead of hurling her weapon at her target anymore, she marched over and forced its point into the wood. Defiantly, with her forbidden left hand, she stabbed the effigy of Sir Eustace Alistair, Baronet.

Chapter the First

October 1889

Alighting from my cab on that sunny October day, I felt an extraordinary sense of well-being. My new calling cards had finally arrived from the printer, and they bore my very own name, Enola Holmes. Wearing my brand-new, cherry-red "polonaise" style jacket, I was going calling on my best friend, and we had a great deal to talk about. Much had happened since the last time I had seen her, several months before.

First and foremost, I was no longer a fugitive from my older brothers, Sherlock and Mycroft Holmes. Since that fateful July day when my mother had disappeared, over a year ago, they had been trying to take me in hand, send me to finishing school, et cetera, and I had been running away from them. But, due to my adventures—indeed, my coups—during that time, they had made peace with me and agreed that I—Enola Eudoria Hadassah Holmes!—was quite capable of living on my own even though I was not yet of legal age.

Also and furthermore, all three of us together, we had learned the whereabouts of our mother. She had conveyed to us a most elucidating letter saying that she was now deceased, and she had known she had not long to live, but she had gone away to spend her last days in peace, beyond the clutches of society's dictates. She lay in an unmarked grave, and we were not to wear any ridiculous and ritualistic black mourning garments for her.

In consequence of all this—reconciling with my brothers at the same time as losing my mother—I had paused to take a breath, so to speak, in my youthful but eventful life. I now boarded in a room at the Professional Women's Club, where even my brother Mycroft had to admit I was perfectly safe, as no males were allowed on the premises. And I had put off practicing as a "Scientific Perditorian," a finder of things lost, until the future. No longer spending my days at "Dr. Ragostin's" office, I was instead taking classes at the London Women's Academy, where I particularly enjoyed the challenges of algebra, geometry, and natural philosophy. Even more, I enjoyed socializing, or perhaps I should say fraternizing, with my brothers, especially Sherlock. Getting to know him better was a particularly intriguing process.

Also and finally, during this time I quite reveled in shopping. How delightful I found it that the "hourglass figure" had at last gone out of style! Just when I no longer needed to wear hip transformers and bosom enhancers to disguise me from my brothers, they were no longer required anyway! On this particular day, I had made the rounds of the dress shops in London with my new friends Tish and Flossie, I had purchased a very modern outfit that disguised me as no one but my slender self, and now I wanted only reunion with my very best friend, Lady Cecily Alistair, to complete my happiness.

Yes, indeed, somehow she was my very best friend even though I had only met her twice, last January and last May . . . well, three times, if one insisted on including the encounter in the lavatory.

———————

Sashaying up the Alistairs' fancy-brickwork walk, I rapped a cheerful rat-a-tat-tat with the front door knocker.

After what seemed like a longish time, the customary stony-faced butler opened the door. Proffering my card, I directed more than asked, "Is Lady Cecily in?"

"Lady Cecily is not seeing anyone." He started to close the door.

"Wait!" I stepped forwards, one foot inside the mansion to prevent him. Surely, even if she was napping, Cecily would not wish to miss my visit. I told the butler, "Take up my card and we shall see."

But without reaching for his salver, he repeated, his tone adamant, "Lady Cecily is seeing *no one.*"

The sun continued to shine—a rare event in London, especially in the autumn—but I felt chilled and shadowed for Lady Cecily's sake. What could be the matter? Having the upper-class misfortune of being born left-handed, Lady Cecily had experienced an even more draconian upbringing than most such girls, being moulded into a demure and docile *right-handed* ornament for society. But, secretly, she had rebelled by boldly sketching in charcoal with her left hand, and she had developed two quite different handwritings. And two personalities: one sweet and ladylike, the other a social reformer. Had she revealed her views to her parents; was she in trouble for that? Or was something more sinister going on? I had been unhappily surprised when I had heard that Cecily's mother had returned to London to reconcile with her husband. Was "reconcile" perhaps not the exact right word?

I told the stone-faced butler, "In that case, I would like a word with Lady Theodora." Once more I offered my card.

Once more he ignored it. "Her Ladyship is seeing no one."

What in the world? Lady Theodora, not entertaining callers? Something was wrong.

"Heavens to Mehitabel!" I exclaimed, becoming wrought. "You know quite well she will see *me*. Do you not remember me?" By rounding and narrowing my shoulders, lowering my head, addressing the floor, and speaking like a well-bred sparrow, I became "Mrs. Ragostin," who had befriended Lady Theodora in a time of crisis. "Do you not remember me?" I repeated in a bitty birdy voice before I straightened to glare at the butler from under my straw hat brim. "Well?" I barked.

I suppose my performance must have shaken him, for his carved-in-marble facade cracked and his demeanor crumbled. "Miss, um, Ragostin, Mrs. I mean, what I've been instructed is nobody gets in, begging your pardon, by Sir Eustace's strict orders." Crisp intonations had deserted him. "I dasn't so much as touch your card, missus, or I could lose my place."

"Sir Eustace's orders!" I echoed, aghast, with my kid-gloved hands to my mouth, for I had heard nothing complimentary and much that was deplorable about Lady Cecily's father.

The poor butler actually flinched. "Oh, no, miss, I didn't mean to say—"

But I did not stay to hear what he didn't mean to say. Dazed and alarmed, I turned, walked down the steps and out to the pavement where a hansom cab awaited me at the kerb.

From his lofty perch, the driver took the unusual

liberty of expressing concern. "Rum go, Miss Enola?" A favourite of mine because he had once loaned me his cab and his exceedingly capable horse, Brownie, he had become my regular cabdriver.

"Rum, indeed, Harold," I told him. He called himself "'Arry," but I titled him Harold. "Please take me home."

From hearing this exchange, the Alistairs' butler may have concluded, if he was listening, that he had disposed of me. If so, then he was much deluded. I had every intention of seeing and speaking with Lady Cecily by whatever means possible before another day had passed.

Seated in the hansom, I smoothed my fashionably narrow skirt and sighed. The outfit I wore had *no* pockets and only a button-up bosom in which to stow supplies for contingencies. Never would I have dreamed I'd ever miss overskirts, bustles, panniers, and all the storage space concealed thereby! I was going to need to develop new safeguards for sleuthing.

———

Once back home at the Professional Women's Club, I did not immediately retire to the chamber upstairs where I lodged. Instead, unbuttoning my polonaise, taking off my hat and swinging it by its ribbons to give an appearance of idleness, I strolled through the reading room and the library, smiling at women who looked up at me. The gentle reader must understand this was London's, and perhaps the world's, first exclusive club for females only. Once secure within its citadel, we could relax without fear of predatory males or society's protocols; other members smiled back at me even if we had not been introduced.

Having not yet located the person I sought, I continued, nodding at women I recognized, through the tea room with its delicate Japanese-style furnishings, then through the card room, and so into a cheerful chintz-draped sitting room, where I saw her standing near a window: a tall, elderly lady who had interested me deeply since the first time I saw her.

She would not have gone unnoticed in any surroundings on account of her toilette: a soft, sunflower-yellow "Aesthetic" gown draping her from her shoulders to her slippers and her long grey hair streaming loose down her back. I did not know her name, but I quite wanted to become acquainted with her because I had overheard her chatting with her exceedingly cultured friends about my mother.

She had known Mum.

So I wanted to know her, although I did not yet wish to reveal who I was—because if I told her my last name, then I would have to report that Mum was deceased, when what was the harm of letting people think that Lady Eudoria Vernet Holmes was vital and free and enjoying life to the fullest somewhere?

This was the first time I had happened upon the tall woman in the loose, flowing gown by herself, which made her easier to approach, although I felt as shy as a child. "Please excuse me for intruding," I ventured.

She turned, quite lithely for one so old, to scrutinize me with the most extraordinary large eyes of celadon green—but no, I realized with mingled shock and glee, her eyes *looked* large and jade-coloured because she had used Spanish papers or something of the sort upon them. How daring! But the forbidden facial emollients were not wasted upon her, for even with her parchment-like skin pleated over the bones of her face, she was strikingly beautiful.

"Why hello, dear." She smiled. "I've seen you about."

Her smile grew puzzled. "But you are looking younger than before."

"Yes," I agreed, "when I came here last May, I was being a married woman in my twenties."

"You 'were being'? Do please explain yourself!" She perched on a camel-back chintz love seat and patted the place next to her for me to sit. "Dear me, there has been a great deal of speculation about Mrs. John Jacobson's marriage, and you mean to topple it all by saying you are not she?"

"Quite so. I am not married." Sitting next to her, I looked up at her. "Please, may I ask what is your name?"

"Oh, how stupid of me not to tell you at once! I am Lady Vienna Steadwell, dear."

Not sure I had heard correctly, I must have frowned.

"Yes, Vienna," she said, her smile ever widening, shirring her thin face. "I was named after the place I was born in, like Florence Nightingale, you know. It must have been a fad of creative parents at the time."

"Much as my creative mother named me Enola." Thus, I managed to tell her my name in part and in passing. I held out my hand. "How do you do, Lady Vienna Steadwell?"

After shaking my hand warmly, Lady Vienna started to ask me something more about myself, but just then the maid entered. Servants, in my experience, possess an uncanny knack for appearing at just the wrong time, but not in this case. Gratefully, I saw the girl coming in with watercress sandwiches, macaroons, and a pitcher of lemonade. As she served, I made quite a point of complimenting her on her simple floral-print dress. Maids at the Women's Club were not required to wear the usual black dress and white apron with ruffled yoke, plus an absurd starched cap that stood up like a wren's tail.

As I had hoped, Lady Steadwell then spoke of dress reform while we devoured sandwiches and macaroons, and I took the chance to tell her how much I liked her unconventional Aesthetic clothing. But she was no fool. Eventually, peering at me, she asked, "Miss Enola, how on earth do you come to be living here, alone, in London at your age?"

"My family lives not far away." True, if evasive; Mycroft and Sherlock were my family.

"Indeed? And what do you do with your days, besides shopping?"

Not minding a bit of teasing, I smiled. "I have been taking a few classes at the Women's Academy."

"Aha!" She quite approved. "Classes in what field of study?"

"A variety. My life's goal is to be a Scientific Perditorian: one who looks for missing persons and things."

"How very extraordinary!"

Her smile and her eyebrows expressed perplexity, but I soldiered on. "In fact, I have a troublesome problem in hand right now, and I hope you won't think me impertinent. . . ." At last I had reached the point where I could pose the question I needed to ask her. "Lady Steadwell, do you happen to be acquainted with the Alistairs?"

She blinked only a few times before answering. "I was, when they were living. But—the Alistair children, you mean? Otelia, Aquilla, and Eustace?"

Children? They were quite my seniors. "Sir Eustace Alistair and his family."

"I am not on familiar terms with any of them, but, of course, I know *of* them. One hears the most deplorable things of them." She sounded a bit prim; evidently, she did not relish gossip.

But I very much wanted to know those deplorable things. "For instance?"

"Oh, for instance, Lady Theodora married Sir Eustace in a fit of martyrdom after having her heart broken by another, and she has been regretting it ever since."

I pretended ignorance. "Sir Eustace is not a good husband?"

"He is not much inferior to the ordinary run of husbands," said Lady Vienna wryly, but then she put down her teacup and spoke more seriously. "Even beyond having his share of the usual masculine flaws, Eustace is short, plump, aspires to a higher station, and altogether has quite a full-blown Napoleon complex."

Now I was ignorant. "Napoleon complex?"

"That is what the alienists call it when a man looks and behaves like a bantam rooster."

"Ah. The alienists," I echoed.

"Yes, the founders of a new science of human behaviour. You have heard about their remarkable studies?"

"Yes." Of which Lady Cecily, with her dual personality, would have been a worthy subject.

"The Napoleon complex," Lady Vienna continued, "is a characteristic form of inferiority complex developed in short men. Sir Eustace exhibits classic symptoms: strutting, posturing, bellowing, being opinionated to the point of megalomania, establishing absolute tyranny over his household."

"Lady Steadwell." Pushing aside the tea tray, I leaned towards her, closing the distance between us and giving her my steady regard. "In your judgment, is Sir Eustace Alistair capable of imprisoning his wife and daughter within their own home?"

Her level gaze never left mine as she replied with blessed simplicity, "Oh, yes."

Chapter the Second

Yes, Cecily was very likely confined to her chamber. Although the thought made me feel ill, such was my conclusion. But there was nothing I could do about it for several anxious hours, until the sun went down.

At dinnertime, however, I continued my research.

Dinner at the Professional Women's Club was not so much a formal affair as a symbolic insurrection against society's solemn strictures. Although the tablecloth was the usual snowy linen, upon its starched surface no two candlesticks matched, and the dozen or more places were set with riotously mixed (although never chipped) fine china. Also, no two pieces of silverware were of the same pattern. Even the napkins enjoyed variety. And—the most revolutionary iconoclasm of all—we women who dined were not required to "dress," meaning make ourselves ornamental for no conceivable reason; instead, we wore whatever we liked so long as it covered our nakedness.

Conversation, also, was far from formal, and as soon as the soup was served this evening, I did not hesitate to tell the others, with spirit and some humour, how unceremoniously I had been turned away from Sir Eustace Alistair's door.

"Heavens, I am shocked but not surprised," responded a matronly club member who wrote an advice column for a weekly newspaper. "The good baronet has always been the most thoroughgoing bully."

"An utter bugbear," agreed a woman who worked as a manager in a department store. "A humbug, his head swollen with putrefying grandiosity, all the more so because he's a mere 'Sir.'"

"Whereas his sisters, Otelia and Aquilla, married 'My Lords' and will never let baby brother Eustace forget it," added a younger woman who happened to be a specialist in ice-water hydrotherapy.

The advice columnist chose to summarize. "Sir Eustace Alistair is a dreadful domestic tyrant. Lady Theodora should have left him long ago, before she bore him so many children."

"One of us should have slipped her a diaphragm," remarked Lady Vienna.

I had no idea what this meant, and other women cast shocked glances, so I did not ask. There was a small, uncomfortable silence.

Without the slightest change in her slightly smiling expression, Lady Vienna added, "I utterly sympathize with her. How dreary it is that she has been forced to return to him."

All of us around the table responded with a murmur of warm agreement as we turned our attention to quail fricassee on rice.

A consulting phrenologist ventured to say in questioning tones, "Lady Theodora was not a woman wronged in the conventional sense of the word. . . ."

"Perhaps not," said the hydrotherapist icily, "but it

is every woman's moral duty to stand up against brow-beating! Why, Sir Eustace was such a tyrant as to hand off his own daughter to his odious sisters to hold captive in starvation, trying to force her to marry her toad of a cousin!"

This I already knew quite well, for it was I who had rescued Cecily by cropping her hair and disguising her as an orphan so that she could escape. And it was my brother Sherlock who had returned her to her mother, who was, at that time, safe with cousins in Devonshire, where I had hoped she would remain.

I said, "It's a shame Lady Theodora's family did not stand up for *her* with more fortitude."

"Financial fortitude is difficult," responded the advice columnist wryly, "and eight children are a great many to feed, no matter how well-off one's family is."

"Which is exactly why we so desperately needed the Women's Property Act!" declared Lady Vienna with bugles ringing in her voice.

"Yes!" several other voices fiercely agreed, and talk then turned to the long-awaited Act, finally passed in 1882, a mere seven years ago. The Act of Parliament had allowed married women to have lands, bank accounts, and so forth of their own, whereas previously everything, even a wife's income from sewing or the like, had legally belonged to the husband. But this righteous Act had been enacted too late for Lady Theodora Alistair. Without any funds of her own, with no way to feed and clothe her children, Lady Theodora had been forced to return to her ogre of a husband.

I grew abstracted towards the end of dinner and bid the others adieu before dessert was served. Returning to my room, I locked the door, then explored my wardrobe for something dark and nondescript to wear. I found a dull brown suit with matching hat, boots, and gloves, which I had wisely kept even though my brothers, especially Mycroft, wished to think my days of stealth, deception, and disguise were over.

Little did they know.

Thus clad, head-covered, and gloved, I slipped out of my chamber and down a back stairway to one of the excellent facilities provided by my club: a Physical Culture Boudoir. Here, in the complete privacy of a large, windowless cellar, members could practice a variety of health-improving rigours for which equipment was provided—parallel bars, Indian clubs, fencing masks and foils, five-pound dumbbells, badminton racquets, inflated rubber balls, et cetera. But, at this hour, as I quite hoped and expected, no one was there.

By the discreet light of a candle I had brought with me, I entered the equipment pantry and selected a bow and some arrows—not deadly weapons by any means, for they lacked tips, being meant for shooting into a straw target.

I intended them for quite another purpose. But how to transport them from here to the Alistair residence without attracting unwanted attention? They most certainly did not fit into the carpetbag in which I carried other items I thought I might need.

Hmm.

Poking about, I found a baritsu cloak in which to wrap the bow and arrows. (Self-defense by baritsu, an Oriental technique, required a gentleman to use only his walking stick and overcoat. Lacking those accoutrements, women practiced with parasols and cloaks.) Thus swaddled, they became merely a bulky but lightweight bundle I could carry under one arm.

And so I sallied forth into a dark and chilly October night. Having sent a messenger for Harold, I found him, his hansom, and the faithful Brownie awaiting me. The cabbie saluted me by touching his hat brim, or as he would say, 'is 'at brim. "Where to, Miss Enola?"

"You remember where you took me earlier today?"

"Yes, miss." His tone reproached me. Of course he remembered.

"Very well. But this time, take me to the rear rather than the front." I quite needed not to be seen by anyone in the house.

"Wot'hever you say, Miss Enola."

On my way, with a chill wind in my face, I mentally attempted in similarly cold logic to review my scheme. In fact, I evaluated it several times, and each time it seemed more unlikely. Still, not long ago I had succeeded in a far more insane enterprise. So finally, massaging my cold, protuberant nose, I set my doubts aside.

The panel in the roof of the cab slid open; Harold wanted to speak with me. "Shall I turn 'ere, Miss Enola?"

I peered into darkness mitigated only slightly by reflected streetlamp light. "By all means, if you would be so good."

"'Ere" was a sloppy back alley that led into a laby-
rinth of mews redolent of carriage horses and manure
piles accumulating at fifty pounds per day per horse.
Fortunately, the stately Alistair home stood taller than
the rest, and I readily recognized its silhouette. Peering
over the roofs of stables and carriage houses, I spied
the back of that four-storey edifice and knocked on the
hansom's roof.

The cab pulled to a halt. "Do you want me to wait,
Miss Enola?"

"No, thank you. I shall be quite all right on my
own." Indeed, after emerging and paying Harold, I
stood where I was until he had gone.

Then, keeping to the shadows, I made my way to a
vantage point behind the Alistair carriage house to survey the back of the Alistair manse. From there, I could
quite clearly see Lady Cecily's bedroom windows—well
known to me from previous visits—by the glare of gaslight within. Each of those windows stood wide open,
of course; if well bred, for the sake of one's aristocratic
health, one must have fresh air while sleeping, no matter how chilly the night might be. But those open windows stood oh so far above me.

In such a wealthy city home, you see, the cellar and ground floor are used for laundry, kitchen, and the like, except for an entrance hall and grand staircase. Elevated above street dust and noise in the first storey are morning room, library, dining room, billiards room, parlour large enough for dancing, et cetera. On the second storey one will find Sir Eustace's chambers and Lady Theodora's boudoir. The third and fourth storeys are for the children: their nursery, schoolroom, and bedchambers. The fourth-storey lights were on and the windows open; no doubt a dutiful nanny was getting the youngest Alistairs—the few who had not yet gone to boarding school—ready for bed. In the attic lodged the servants.

As I crouched in a narrow, well-shadowed space between the carriage house and the hedge, unwrapping my bow and arrows, I saw a familiar form pass behind Cecily's third-floor windows. As I had presumed, she was in her room.

From my carpetbag, I took a ball of slender string manufactured for the flying of kites. After unrolling quantities of it, I tied its end securely to one of my arrows just above the feathers.

Although hardly an expert, I had shot arrows before; archery was a common pastime for girls raised in the country. I felt reasonably confident that, in order to attract Cecily's attention, I could zing an arrow through her open window—a window far too high for me to reach by other means, such as the time-honoured method of throwing pebbles.

Carefully surveying the premises for stable boys, kitchen help, or any other such stragglers, I saw none. Just the same, my heart beat faster as I stepped into the open. Surely, in my dark costume I blended into the gloom of night . . . but even so, as no one raised an alarm, it took me a long moment to breathe out. Nocking my arrow to the bowstring, I lifted my bow, drew it to my utmost, and shot my arrow at a high angle calculated to send it soaring into Cecily's window.

Alas, it did nothing of the sort. Instead, whether because of the dragging kite string or my lack of skill or sheerest perversity, it skittered off in a decidedly unfortunate sideways direction to bang smartly against a window on the second storey.

"What the h— was that?" bellowed a peremptory

masculine voice that, employing such naughty language, could have belonged only to Sir Eustace.

My arrow fell to the ground beside the mansion. Ducking back into the shadows of the carriage house, I pulled in the kite string hand over hand, with frenzied rapidity retrieving the guilty evidence. I was still reeling it in when I heard the front door slam, and four men in evening dress came careening around the corner of the mansion towards me. One was the butler. Two might have been guests. But the one in the lead, carrying a lantern, was unmistakably Sir Eustace.

Unmistakably—even though I had never seen him before—because he bore a close resemblance to his harridan sisters, with whom I was unfortunately acquainted. Like Aquilla and Otelia, Eustace had pursy little features centred in a broad and fleshy face: button eyes; a compressed, babyish mouth; and even a pug nose. Also like Aquilla and Otelia, he had a marked excess of girth.

"I saw something move over there!" he roared, pointing towards my hiding place.

Chapter the Third

In such moments of exigency, even the most timely re-action seems to take forever. In this case, I needed to hide carpetbag, baritsu cloak, bow, arrows, and most urgently, myself. Would that I could have done all of the above in an instant! But no; by the time I had thrust my bow and arrows through the hedge and shoved my carpetbag after them, the men were nearly upon me. Bundling the baritsu cloak in my arms, I scuttled back between the carriage house and the hedge like a cock-roach into a crack. Just as the lantern shone upon the place where I had been, I whisked around the corner of the carriage house and flattened my back against it, panting. The logical thing to do would have been to run away into the mews.

Logic isn't everything.

Sidling to the other end of the carriage house, I peeked around the corner, hoping I would see the men going back to their game of billiards or whatever they had been doing.

Instead, I saw a slender, petite, and graceful girl in a nightgown looking out of a lofty window.

Cecily!

I leapt out from behind the carriage house and waved at her.

Her head alerted like that of a startled deer. She saw me.

But so did Sir Eustace. "You!" he roared.

Even when I must hold a bundled cloak with one hand and yank my skirt above my knees with the other, I can still run faster than most people, and I did so. I dashed off, and, shouting like a pack of hounds, the men followed me. I led them into the murky nighttime obscurity of the mews, dodged around the corner of a stable, ran past a manure bin and a chicken coop, then turned towards a goat pen. Goats are great climbers and so am I. Tossing my cloak atop the goat shed, up I went after it, then onto the next, higher rooftop—perhaps a creamery? It was hard to tell, and I cared not. On that mossy, quaint rooftop I lay flat, cloak and all, and froze like a hare in a thicket lest I loosen a slate, send it clattering down, and give myself away.

Within a moment, quite a number of men stampeded in my direction. I tried to hold my breath but could not stop panting. It didn't matter; panting themselves, and shouting so they could not possibly have heard me, they pounded past me.

The moment I saw their backs, I broke cover, swung down to the ground, and ran back the way I had come, returning to the Alistairs' carriage house. This time, however, rather than slipping behind it, I darted inside, for all the doors hung open; the grooms and stable boys who slept upstairs had gone out to join the chase. It was so dark as to be quite nearly black in there, but my night vision, I am glad to say, is excellent. I made for the fanciest carriage, a phaeton, got into it, and flattened myself beneath its plush seats. As an afterthought, I covered myself with my versatile baritsu cloak, then stayed still, mimicking all the other dark upholstery, hoping to be overlooked if anyone glanced in there.

But no one came near. Presently, I heard the doors being closed and latched, heard the occupants of the loft of the carriage house return to their beds, and eventually, after an hour or so, I heard them start to snore.

I waited another hour or thereabouts, until I felt fairly sure Sir Eustace was also snoring. Then, taking care to make no noise, I crept out of the phaeton and out of the carriage house. Had there been a dog to bark at my departure, I would have been doomed, but perhaps Sir Eustace did not care for dogs.

Certainly, he did not greatly care for his wife or his eldest daughter.

All the windows of the Alistair mansion had gone dark except Lady Cecily's. She was waiting for me, and I knew I must not disappoint her.

Cautiously, quietly, I retrieved my carpetbag and my bow and arrows from the hedge. Fumbling, I located the arrow with the string attached to it. Walking much nearer to Lady Cecily's open bedroom window than before, once more I took aim at that lighted orifice and shot my arrow.

I missed, but not too badly. The arrow tapped against the brick wall.

Muttering something naughty, I tried again.

And missed again.

I will spare the gentle reader an account of the many attempts that followed. Suffice it to say that this could have gone on all night had Cecily not come to the window and leaned out to peer down at me, her entire figure forming a question mark, although, of course, she had the good sense not to utter a word.

I stepped forwards so that she could see me—the only illumination came from her window and, indirectly, streetlamps—and I held up the arrow dangling from the string, which I am sure was invisible to her in the gloom. I stretched the string between my hands, length by length, willing her to understand.

Her mouth formed an *O*, and then she straightened, holding up her forefinger, signaling me to wait. She disappeared from my sight.

Biting my lip, I retreated into the shadows to wait for what seemed an inordinate length of time.

But at last Cecily returned to the window with—my stars and garters! She carried a ball of knitting yarn of some pastel hue. With one hand, she thrust it out the window, and, with the other hand, she began rapidly to unwind it.

Abandoning my bow and arrows, I took my carpetbag and, trying to be as silent as a footpad, stalked forwards to position myself under the window. So deep in the shadow of the manse, I could not see a thing but alternately felt for the descending yarn and groped in my carpetbag for the next item I needed.

The yarn brushed against my nose, naturally; all my life I have tended to encounter things with my proboscis first. Grasping the yarn, I tugged to let Cecily know I had it, then, fumbling over the knot in the dark, I tied to it the end of a hank of stout brown twine.

The yarn, you see, was not strong enough to withstand the weight of a rope—no more so than my kite string would have been.

I tugged again, but Cecily seemed not to understand; nothing happened. I ran back into the light, such as it was, and pantomimed the act of hauling something up.

At once she set to work like a good sailor, and as soon as she had hold of the twine, I signaled her to stop and wait while I went, as stealthily as I could, to attach the concluding item.

The rope.

This time, as soon as I tugged, she hauled it in. Standing once again in my single vantage point of visibility, I waited until she held the rope in her hands, then mimed the act of knotting it, placing great emphasis on drawing the ends tight. She nodded, then disappeared.

I quite hoped she understood that she must fasten it with utmost security to some very sturdy and immobile object in her room so that I could climb up and have a chat with her, stony-faced butler be dashed. I went over to the window and grasped hold of my end, waiting in inky darkness for her signal to ascend.

I felt a tug on the rope, but then, most unexpectedly, it seemed to come alive in my hands, startling me so badly that I nearly let go! The gentle reader must understand that, in utter darkness, feeling the rope jerk this way and that as if of its own volition, I passed a most unpleasant moment before I comprehended that something was coming down the rope towards me. Even then, I could scarcely believe it, for Lady Cecily was not and had never been such a tomboy as I. When her bare foot touched my hand, I almost screamed.

Letting go of the rope as she alighted on the ground, I gasped, "Cecily?" Luckily, surprise had taken my breath away to such an extent that I spoke quite softy.

"Enola," she whispered with tears of passion in her voice, "I must get away at once."

"In your *nightgown?*" A nightgown so white that even in the shadows I could see a kind of ghost of her.

"They took away my clothes. And my books, and anything to write with or paint with. I shall go mad. Enola—" Her voice broke.

I reached out to her, located her hand, held it in mine, and started walking, guiding her towards the mews at a gentle pace while my mind raced.

Very well, Enola. One impossibility at a time.

Skirting the light from Cecily's window, I managed to find my carpetbag, bow, arrows, and baritsu cloak. Only the lattermost item seemed likely to be of any further use. I wrapped its dark folds around Cecily, covering her from neck to ankles in order to make her less conspicuous. From my bosom, or rather my concealed frontal baggage, I got out a dusky shawl to cover

Cecily's bright hair, but as I placed it upon her, my fingers told me that her blond tresses were unfashionably cropped.

"Still so short!" I whispered. I had shorn her hair to disguise her as an orphan the most recent time I had needed to rescue her, but that was months ago.

"I cut it off again when Father bludgeoned us back home, and nearly gave him apoplexy. I knew he had waited until it grew out only to auction me off for marriage to the highest bidder."

Abandoning bow, arrows, rope, carpetbag, et cetera to the fates, I led Cecily back past the carriage house. "I suppose your parents then took away your scissors, as well."

"It's just Father. I don't know . . ." Her voice quavered. "I haven't heard from Mother at all since Father locked me up."

"But surely her maid could tell you—"

"I am allowed no conversation with the servants."

"Dreadful," I murmured. With no idea where we were going or how best to get there, I took Cecily out to the alley, where I chose my direction at random; we walked eastwards. Within a few moments, I felt Cecily start to shiver in the cold, and limp as stones hurt her feet.

"If you can make it to the next cross street," I told her softly, "the pavement will be smoother. And there will be streetlights. You will be able to see the stones."

But I did not say the rest of what I was thinking, confound this impromptu escapade not properly planned. The one place where I might be able to hide Cecily was on the far side of the city. In no way could we walk there even if she were not barefoot. Yet, if I hailed a cab for us, we were sure to be noticed and traced. Trams, omnibuses, and the underground did not run at this time of night. Yet, even if it were not so cold, we could not possibly stop so close to the Alistair residence to wait for daylight.

Our progress became slower with every step. We had not yet reached a pavement.

I said to Lady Cecily, "Let me carry you on my back."

"Enola! I couldn't possibly!"

"Yes, you could and we must. Your feet are bleeding, are they not?"

"I cannot see."

"If not now, then they soon will be, and you will leave a plain trail for anyone to follow." I put my back to her and crouched. "You're as light as a child. Up you go."

"Enola—"

"Hands around my neck and *up*," I ordered in a commanding tone worthy of the sister of Sherlock Holmes. Cecily obeyed, and as she hopped, I caught her behind the knees and hoisted her. Then, with her lower limbs (females never admit to having legs) dangling over my arms, off we went, borne by my booted feet, making far better speed.

She weighed so little that I demanded, "Have they been starving you again?"

She didn't answer, only laid her head down. I felt tears against the back of my neck.

But she would not cry out loud. Both of us remained silent for some time, during which I strode a distance of several blocks. All of my limbs and several other portions of my anatomy started to ache. Bent over, I began to see only the ground in front of me and think only of completing my next stride. In short, I became quite lacking in vigilance.

"'Ello!" called an authoritative voice quite close at hand. "Wot's going on 'ere?"

Chapter the Fourth

A uniformed constable making his rounds lifted his lantern to survey us.

"Git ye dowun, Katie me dear," I told Cecily in an Irish accent, the better to blarney with. Under the circumstances and in my nondescript costume, my own aristocratic accent would have been suspect. "Sure and it's after finding me wee sister I am," I lilted to the constable, greatly relieved to be standing upright, while Cecily played her part by clinging to my arm like a child, "and her likely to spind the night on the streets, the divil take thim as bore her away for the sake uv tuppence ha'penny and stole her shoes intirely. And it's takin' her home to a warum bed and a sup o' soup, I am, if all the blissid saints be willing. And—"

"'Ome to where?" interrupted the constable with an admirable grasp of the essential.

"Sure and it's clear to Sivin Dials I must be carrying her." Seven Dials was an unsavoury neighbourhood near my destination. "And it be so cold, and her poor feet all raddled wit blood."

"I can see that," grumbled the constable with the scowl of a busy man obliged to do a kindness. "Come along." He strode off towards a street corner call box. We followed. I let Cecily limp along because we needed to fall behind him so I could whisper to her. "Don't say a word," I breathed close to her ear. It was too much to expect that she should talk like an Irish colleen.

The constable opened the box with a key and cranked at the instrument within.

"Is that a telephone?" Cecily blurted, evidently so excited she forgot my warning.

"Shh!" I told her.

Thanks to the noise of his cranking, the constable

reacted to the sound of our voices only by giving us an inquiring look.

"Be that a tillyphone?" I said in response.

"Sure an 'tis." My Irish accent was infecting the constable. "Aven't you never seed one before? Hit's a hofficial *police* tillyphone." Then he talked into the mouthpiece. "'Ello? 'Ello! I need you to send a hofficer wit a 'orse up 'ere. Wot for? For to take two girls 'ome, one before and one behind."

Accursed kindness! The last thing Cecily and I needed was this much attention.

"Wait a minute, 'old on," said the "hofficer" to the telephone, and he left the listening device dangling by its wire as he sallied into the street. Evidently, he had recognized a clip-clop I also heard approaching.

"I would *love* to subscribe to a telephone," Cecily whispered. "Aunt Otelia has one."

"Would you *hush*?" I whispered back.

Meanwhile, the constable yelled, "'Alloo!" and windmilled with both arms, reminding me that one code I had not yet learned was semaphore, or "wigwag" as the sailors called it. I made a mental note: *Learn semaphore.*

Teach Cecily. If the past predicts the future, we will need it. We certainly could have used some means of communication when I was standing in her backyard.

From out of the shadows beyond the streetlamps appeared a swaybacked old horse driven by a hunched and shabby man, a costermonger, by the evidence of his shapeless hat and clothing, seated in a rickety wagon.

"'Alloo yerself, Jeffries," he replied to the constable.

"Good morning, Lucas. Yer up early. Going to Billingsgate?"

"Where else?"

The man was cheeky, but the constable seemed not to care. He thumbed over his shoulder towards where Cecily and I stood huddled together on the pavement. "If ye'd take these two as far as Seven Dials, I'll be obliged."

The costermonger gave no more answer than a growl. But, without further ceremony, the constable turned, seized me by what should have been my waist if I had one, lifted me, and thumped me into the wagon, where I sat in the straw with my mouth open as he deposited Cecily beside me. I retained just enough wit to be glad to see she had ducked her head to keep her face hidden in the shadow of her shawl.

"Lie down," I whispered to her as the horse walked on. "Pretend to sleep." And, burrowing into the straw for warmth, I did likewise, rather than calling "A thousand thanks to yerself!" to the constable. I wanted neither him nor the costermonger to recall us very clearly.

"Where are we?" Cecily asked as I opened the hidden door behind the concealing evergreen bush, its latch operated by pressing a certain curlicue in the "gingerbread" woodwork.

"Shh." We'd arrived at my destination just at dawn. Mrs. Bailey would be up and about in the kitchen, which could prove awkward, as both Cecily and I quite wanted something to eat.

With this problem in mind, I failed to notice at first that Cecily's voice sounded wispy and meek.

The secret door swung open quite silently upon its well-oiled hinges, admitting us to the inner office of the house I provided for "Dr. Leslie Ragostin, Perditorian."

Although "Dr. Ragostin" had curtailed his business hours until further notice, I remained in possession of the premises, receiving rents from the boarders overhead.

Once I had closed the door behind us, causing it to become, in appearance, nothing more than a bookshelf, I guided Cecily to the davenport where so many times I had swaddled myself in afghans and napped. On that comfortable couch, I seated her. Looking dazed, she glanced around at Dr. Ragostin's huge mahogany desk, the Turkey carpet, the heavily draped windows on walls otherwise lined by bookshelves. And the gas chandelier, which I must not light because Joddy, the boy-in-buttons, might notice its gleam under the door. But, to eyes that had been open all night, there was sufficient illumination in the gloom.

I tiptoed across the room, cautioned Cecily with a finger to my lips, then swung open another bookshelf to reveal a small, secret room. This cubbyhole, once used to deceive the gullible during séances, was where I kept the various clothing, wigs, hats, and such I required for disguises, along with buckets of water for washing away face paint and the like.

First and foremost, I needed this water. Partially

filling a basin, I added a goodly amount of tincture of arnica from a bottle I kept handy, then carried my makeshift restorative to Cecily, placing it on the floor and guiding her feet into it. The water was unheated, of course, but Cecily hardly seemed to notice it. Perched on the edge of the davenport with her shoulders pitifully hunched, she whispered, "Where am I?"

A mouse could have squeaked with more force of character. Trying not to frown, I studied her, then went to "Dr. Ragostin's" desk, found paper, and wrote the house's address on it. Returning, I offered this to Cecily. "Here."

She reached out to take it with her *right hand.*

Ye gods. How had she and *when* had she turned from a left-handed rebel into her submissive other self?

"Cecily," I demanded, albeit keeping my voice low, "when you climbed down the rope, were you right-handed?"

Her eyes widened, childlike. "I beg your pardon?"

"When you climbed out of your bedroom window—"

With utmost courtesy she reached out confidingly—and, alas, with her right hand—to touch my arm and halt my questioning. "There has been some sort of absurd mistake," she told me gently. "I have never climbed out of a window or down a rope in my life."

"You don't remember?"

"The last thing I remember is going to bed, so how did I come here?"

My mind gibbered like a monkey in the zoo, but I somehow managed to keep my voice soft. "But you do remember that they locked you in your room and were starving you?"

Her face winced as if I had hurt her, but she whispered, "Yes."

"So we must hide you."

"Yes."

"This is the hiding place where I have brought you. It has been a long night. Once you've had a good meal and a sleep, it will all come back to you."

Or so I hoped! All, including the vital principle embodied in her left hand!

"You stretch out on the davenport," I murmured in soothing tones as I fetched a couple of thick crocheted afghans and spread them over her, tucking them in around her poor, cold feet. "I will go get us something to eat."

Confound this unplanned rescue. This room was kept locked, and I had the key; Cecily would be quite safe here, even from Mrs. Fitzsimmons, the housekeeper—but if Cecily and I were to eat, I had to sally forth and order breakfast. The clothes I was wearing would never do; I had to change into something more seemly for the mistress of this household to wear.

Sighing with worry, I retired to the secret room to do so, with a candle for light and the door open so Cecily could see where I was. I had hoped never again to wear a skirt with its hem dragging on the ground, but I had no dresses of recent fashion available to me, so on it went. And I had hoped I would never again need to wear a wig, blasted heavy thing, but the hat that matched the dress was permanently attached atop one, so on it went, as well. Once clad in this rich but tasteful dove-grey ensemble, rolling my eyes, I emerged.

Cecily peered up at me from the davenport like a mouse at a cat. I made a comical face, but she didn't smile or laugh. Bending down, I whispered close to her ear: "I should be back in a little while."

Then I exited by the secret door—and so that no one, especially not my own cook and housekeeper, would learn of its existence, I took cover in the topiary garden of the house next door, passed through it to the carriage entrance in the rear, and walked around the block to approach my own property from the pavement, holding the key to the front door in my kid-gloved hand.

However, no sooner had I surmounted the brick porch with its elaborate white wooden filigree, no sooner did I stop in front of the oak door, preparing to let myself in, than I saw the shadow of a tall man in a top hat encroaching.

Even before I turned to face him, I knew who it was.

And even though I wore my wig and quite a dressy costume, he knew who I was.

He spanned the three porch steps with a single stride and stood looming over me quite without any brotherly smile. "Enola," demanded Sherlock Holmes in his most peremptory tone, "what have you done with Lady Cecily Alistair?"

Chapter the Fifth

I did not need to pretend surprise. I *was* surprised, and able to respond with convincing imbecility, because nobody should have missed Cecily until morning, least of all Sherlock Holmes.

"Cecily?" I repeated, and then with an admirable show of alarm, "Has something happened to *Cecily?*"

"Has something happened to Cecily?" he mimicked in a puerile fashion quite unworthy of the Great Detective. Or of any adult, for that matter, unless he happened to be my brother. . . . Turning my back to hide my smile, I applied my key to the door, opened it, and let myself in. Following me, Sherlock complained, "You know quite well what has happened to her."

"*Au contraire,* I am breathlessly anxious to hear." After pulling the bell rope to summon my boy-in-buttons, I sat in an overstuffed armchair just outside "Dr. Ragostin's" office so that Cecily, nestled on the davenport within, would be sure to hear every word, and I gestured for Sherlock to be seated in the chair next to mine. However, ignoring my mute invitation, he paced instead.

Very well; he thereby gave me reason to raise my voice. "How do you come to be looking for Lady Cecily, Sherlock?" I fluted.

"Because Lady Theodora had hysterics until I was called in! Roused from my bed at four in the morning!"

Ye gods in holey pyjamas, Cecily's escape must have been discovered almost immediately after she and I departed, perhaps when we were still making our slow way down the alley! My mind gabbled in dismay at what might yet become a disaster, but I kept a smooth face and spoke as if I had very little knowledge of the situation. "And why, pray tell, was Lady Theodora in hysterics?"

Sherlock gave me a furiously baffled look. But my

page boy, Joddy, ran into the room at that moment in answer to my summons, and he quite astonished me by acting like a well-trained servant. Giving no sign that he was surprised to see us there so early, he took Sherlock's hat, gloves, and stick, laid them on the table that stood near the door for that purpose, pulled back the window draperies to let in daylight, then looked to me for further orders.

"My guest and I will partake of breakfast in here, Joddy," I told him.

"Yes, Miss 'Olmes." He ran out again.

"My goodness, Miss Holmes," said Sherlock in a bitingly expressive monotone. "You look very much like the matronly Mrs. Jacobson who used to work here."

"And a darling woman she was. Thank you."

"In the very hat that so exactly goes with that wig."

"Of course."

"And why, pray tell," asked Sherlock, glowering down at me, "did you not partake of breakfast at your club?"

"The food is better here." This was not at all true, but he would never be able to prove otherwise.

"I stopped at the Women's Club before coming here. No one there had seen you."

"Such is the standard reply to all such impertinent inquiries made by males, and seldom a day goes by without any, believe me. How ever did you get in the door?"

"How ever did you get here?" he countered. "I saw no cab."

"By the underground."

"Enola!" Seldom have I seen him so aghast. "You use the *underground*?"

"I always have done, ever since coming to London. Why ever are your eyebrows jumping about in such an alarming fashion? It is just another type of train."

"With carriages shared by the most common and unsavoury people!"

"Just as the streets are. What of it? You have not answered my question. You were not admitted to the Women's Club at all, were you?"

"Only my foot wedged into the door." Sighing, he finally sat down in the chair by my side and studied me with an expression that was, for him, almost quizzical. "Enola, I know you called upon Lady Cecily yesterday."

"Then you also know I was turned away."

"In which case I am sure you were dissatisfied." He leaned towards me, all angles with his elbows on his knees and his fingers steepled. "Now truly, renegade sister of mine, can you possibly expect to convince me that *anyone* other than you would shoot an arrow attached to a string into Lady Cecily's window, then send up a rope in order for her to descend like a monkey?"

I think he was trying to trick me into saying yarn was used, not string, or that I could not hit anything smaller than a church with an arrow. But I dissembled. Leaning forwards as eagerly as he, I demanded, "Is that what all this fanfaronade is about? Has Lady Cecily *run away?*"

"You know quite well—"

"Nonsense! She would never crawl down a rope. I refuse to believe it."

"The rope entered the premises via one of *your* carpetbags."

"Arrant nonsense. Have you devised a method whereby to tell one carpetbag from another, like cigar-ashes?"

He would have replied with another volley, I am sure, but Joddy entered just then with an admirable breakfast tray exhibiting no less than four boiled eggs, in egg-stands, wearing what looked like Turkish hats surmounted by tassels, covers to keep them warm. Along with the eggs came sliced tongue, broiled trout, and hot rolls that gave forth a delectable aroma of butter and cinnamon. Truly, Mrs. Bailey had outdone herself. Even before the boy had situated the tray, I snatched a large napkin and spread it across my frontal regions preparatory to feasting. "You'll join me, I'm sure?" I invited Sherlock quite sincerely.

"I will do nothing of the sort." He rose. "I intend to search these premises."

I am sure he expected vehement protest from me, but I merely waved him on his way with my spoon as I tackled my first egg. Scowling, he strode off to investigate the dining room, the kitchen, the servants' quarters, and, no doubt, the flats upstairs, leaving me alone to eat. I pretended good appetite in case Sherlock was spying, and, for this same reason, I stayed where I was, although I desperately wished to slip into the inner office to check on Cecily. I hoped that, having overheard everything Sherlock had said, she had taken her basin, removed her traces, and hidden herself in the secret room. But having last seen her giving a good imitation of a dormouse . . . My heart hurt with worry for her.

I had finished my second egg and was just applying my linen napkin to my mouth when Sherlock came striding in to stand by "Dr. Ragostin's" sanctum, his aquiline features as hard as ice. "Unlock this door," he told me with great decision.

"Certainly," I said; to refuse would have confirmed his suspicions. Although my heart started pounding hard, I made sure my face showed no misgivings, and I got up with neither haste nor delay to turn the key in the lock. Instantly, Sherlock flung the door open and thrust his way in.

Looking past him, I saw at once, with huge relief, that Cecily was not occupying the davenport.

"What ever happened to 'ladies first'?" I chided my brother as I pocketed the key and followed him in.

He did not respond even with a glance. Rather more forcefully than was necessary he drew back the drapes, letting light into the room, and then he stood glaring from desk to davenport to armchairs and back as if any one of those furnishings might have concealed Lady Cecily.

"A candle has been burned in here," he said with a discomfiting gleam in his eyes.

My pulse speeded alarmingly, but I hoped my voice betrayed no concern as I said, "Surely not." I glanced at the decorative tapers on the mantel over the fireplace, which remained as white and chaste, including their wicks, as the day they were placed there. "What candle?" No others stood in the room. "What makes you think—"

"I *smell* it. And so do you, Enola."

"Heavens, my dear brother, how can you presume to tell me what I smell?" Because I felt oddly reluctant to lie to him, I made light of the matter.

With no softening of his face, however, Sherlock demanded, "Where is the secret room?"

Had I been knocked over by a coach and four, the shock could hardly have been less. I am afraid my face betrayed my consternation as I echoed, "Secret room?"

"Do not trifle with me, Enola. I am not a fool. You think I have forgotten that séances were held here? Of course, there is a secret room. Show it to me at once," he ordered me as if I were a naughty child.

Topsy-turvy, my shock somersaulted into irritation. "Oooh, we must not trifle with the great Sherlock

Holmes," I mocked, flouncing to the davenport, where I plopped myself down, arms crossed. "Find it your famous self."

And so he did, of course, within a few minutes, thumping the walls behind the bookcases until he found the one that sounded hollow, then searching with skilled fingers for the way to open it. Clinging to only the faintest hope that he might not find it, and trying to think what on earth I could do when he did, I sat with my back to him, my teeth clenched and my hands in fists, pretending stubborn indifference.

"Aha!" said Sherlock.

I closed my eyes, despairing for Lady Cecily, yet at the same time hoping that she and I together, pleading her case to Sherlock, might convince him of . . . something, some compromise with her dreadful father, please. . . .

The secret door opened, as I have said, soundlessly. And silence was all I heard for moments, very slow and prolonged moments. When I could no longer bear the waiting, I opened my eyes and turned around to see—

What?

The bookshelf hung open, and within the secret

room, Sherlock had lighted the candle and stood looking about him.

That was all.

But—but where was Cecily?

Chapter the Sixth

Striving my utmost to convey an appearance of calm indifference, I imagine I did not quite succeed. Surely, my face was a study as I joined my brother in the small chamber, more of a closet than a room, where I kept my paraphernalia of disguise. Except for the wardrobe, there was simply nowhere for Lady Cecily to hide. But the wardrobe already stood open. Obviously, Sherlock had inspected it. Now he was studying my shelves and cupboards full of scarves and shawls, boots, stockings, gloves, wigs, hair extensions, hats, and—and *unmentionables!*—as if Lady Cecily might be found concealed behind a corset.

"Are you quite satisfied?" I asked with unfeigned bitterness.

He jumped as if startled out of the deepest cogitations, turning to me. "I beg your pardon!" He sounded as if he meant it. A moment later he added more calmly but no less sincerely, "Enola, it would appear I owe you an apology for this intrusion."

"Just go, please."

"Of course." He hastened to oblige. I closed the secret room behind us and led him out of the office, noticing with mixed feelings that Joddy had taken away the breakfast tray; Lady Cecily remained hungry. At the front door, I stood waiting with scant patience while my brother retrieved his hat, stick, and gloves.

Sherlock studied my face. "Again, my apologies," he said, "but *only* for sullying your secret boudoir with my barbaric masculine presence. Despite my futile search, make no mistake about it, I am as convinced as I was when I entered this door that you had something to do with the disappearance of Lady Cecily Alistair."

For an instant, I badly wanted to take him into my

confidence, and I shook the idea out of my head in a daze, blurting out a partial truth. "I am quite worried about her myself."

"Then I promise you, if I find her, you will be among the first to know." Rather magnanimously, Sherlock extended his gloved hand to me, and I admit I felt easier in my mind about deceiving him because of that gesture.

After I shook his hand, he left.

I watched from a window as my handsome (to my eyes) older brother got into a cab and departed.

But once certain he had gone away and could not see me, I forgot any caution in my frenzy of worry for my lost lady. "Cecily!" Calling her name, I rushed back into "Dr. Ragostin's" sanctum, slamming the door after me and locking it, and then I ran to the secret door that led outside and thrust it open, half hoping and half fearing to find Cecily shivering beneath the evergreen in her nightgown.

But she was not there. And I saw no sign that she ever had been.

I looked up and down the narrow space between houses. Nothing. I started towards the back to check henhouse, garden shed, and other such buildings in case she might be hiding there, but made myself stop after I had taken a few steps. *Enola, think,* Mum's remembered voice told my mind in calming, quelling tones. One must never let the servants see one with one's hair down, so to speak.

And surely Cecily would not hide in a chicken coop in her nightgown or roam the London streets midmorning in one.

More sensibly and quietly, I went back inside, secured the door, then set about looking for any helpful indications.

I was not long in finding some. Inside the secret chamber, Cecily had wisely wrapped her nightgown inside the dark-coloured baritsu cloak before stuffing it under a shelf where it had gone unnoticed even by the famous Sherlock Holmes. Whilst changing clothes that morning, I had unceremoniously jettisoned my old brown suit on the floor; it was no longer there. Just in case Cecily might have ever so tidily hung it up, I checked the wardrobe, but I did not find it there, either. I felt justified in concluding that she had, very sensibly, clothed herself in the mousy-looking suit, shabby and out-of-fashion, in which she would attract no attention whatsoever. She had taken my boots, also, and no doubt had put on double stockings to protect her feet. However, my mannish felt hat remained upside down, flattening its crown, on the shelf where I had thrown it.

I frowned at it as if it had transgressed.

Then my mind cleared, and I forgave it. Of course, Cecily had needed to cover her indecently short hair. Doubtless she had borrowed some sort of wrapper, a scarf or a shawl.

But where had she gone? Would she ever come back? Had she left me no message of explanation or farewell?

Thinking this, I felt suddenly desolate and beyond all reason, crushed by blackest devastation so vast and weighty that tears burned to be released from my eyes.

Enola, this will never do.

I shook my head, shaking away my despair, which was nothing more than déjà vu, an echo of what I had felt a year before when my mother had run away. But I had been a girl then, I had become a woman since, and Cecily was not my mother; she was a friend and I must help her.

Think. Put yourself in her place.

Blinking away my incipient tears, I thought: *I am Cecily, in my nightgown, lying down after having soaked my injured feet in a basin, when I hear Sherlock Holmes come into the building, looking for me. I must fold my blankets, then hide any other traces. What to do first?*

Get rid of the basin.

Where had she put it?

And, of course, the moment I looked for it, I saw it, upside down on a shelf, probably still wet and making a mess. I seized it.

I had not given Cecily sufficient credit for good sense. Obviously she had reverted to her left-handed, resourceful self. Not only had she dried the basin after emptying it into one of my buckets, but she had placed it upside down to conceal something she had left for me.

I clutched this with shaking hands: a sheet of paper from "Dr. Ragostin's" desk, on which she had penciled:

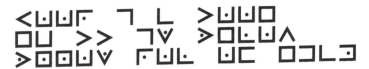

This I understood at once—or thought I did—for the "pigpen" cipher is the simplest of all schoolchildren's secret codes; Cecily and I had used it before. Almost anyone, including Sherlock—no, *especially* Sherlock— could read it as easily as I, and carrying it to the desk to decipher it, I thought Cecily had been a bit reckless in that regard. But he had not seen it, so I shrugged as I sat down. On another sheet of paper I scrawled the key:

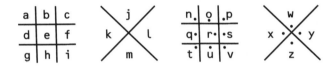

The secret, you see, is to draw the shape of the al- phabet letter's box or container rather than writing the letter itself. So the first letter of Cecily's message had to be L. Then O, then another O, then—V?

Loov?

Unhappy doubts began to shadow my sentiments, but I persevered to the end of the first line.

Loov g ckooe

Obviously, something was wrong. I tried reading it backwards, eookc g vool, and then alternate letters, logko or ovcoe? Scrambled, okgol or eocvo? Simply ridiculous.

The first two letters of the middle line were eb. I tried combining them with letters of the top line to no avail. Did all three lines serpentined together perhaps spell out something?

In brief and after much wasted effort: no, they did not.

So much for the code anyone could easily read.

I will spare the gentle reader details of the mental contortions I performed for the next hour or more as I failed to comprehend Cecily's seemingly oh-so-simple message. By luncheon time, I had grown nearly sufficiently frantic to fly into hysterics as Cecily's mother had reportedly done. How ever was I to proceed? Insofar as I had managed to plan at all, I had thought I would bring Cecily food, then provide her with simple yet elegant clothing, then take her back to the Women's Professional Club with me, where she could stay hidden for an indeterminate length of time until we decided how best to deal with the problems presented by her dictatorial father. Legally, you see, she had no recourse;

yet perhaps morally, or perhaps by means of pressure or persuasion—

But what was I thinking? Lady Cecily was gone, and I had no idea where or whether I would ever see her again!

Chapter the Seventh

"Just when the day seems darkest, one should expect it to go completely black." Such was the current quip from some satirical wit—perhaps Oscar Wilde?—and it all too aptly described, from my point of view, the day Lady Cecily went missing. From terror that Sherlock would find her in the secret room, I progressed, or perhaps I should say regressed, to utmost horror that she had ventured into the teeming cesspool that is London on her own—and what if she turned right-handed again, becoming as helpless as a child? I could not sit still; I circled Dr. Ragostin's office, pacing, as all the terrible things that might be happening to Cecily whirled like a nightmare carousel in my mind. Cecily run over by a tram, Cecily in the workhouse picking oakum until her fair hands bled, Cecily bullied by male pests, Cecily starving in some foul alley, Cecily seized by white slavers and forced into a life of depravity, Cecily disguising herself as a boy only to be arrested as a pickpocket and thrown in gaol—

Just as I felt that I would go quite mad and spin like a dervish, a thought seized me, almost literally grabbing me by the throat with such force that I halted in the middle of the Turkey carpet and stood still:

Mishaps of this sort were exactly what Sherlock had feared for me a mere year ago, when I had run away.

And how nonsensical his thinking had seemed to me then! Now, however, for the first time I realized how greatly concerned for me he must have been, and I felt such a surge of affection for him that, beset with a mubble-fubble of emotions as I was, I actually burst into tears. I collapsed onto the davenport, applied my face to one of its plush pillows, and sobbed until—?

Hours later I woke up.

Having never previously cried myself to sleep, at first I could make no sense of anything, especially not the crusty, sticky feeling around my eyes and nose. I observed the mess I had made on the plush cushion, gave quite a naughty exclamation, and hastened for water to cleanse it and myself. But despite such outward disorder, I found myself inwardly a bit better regulated. While I quite wanted to find Cecily and feared severe consequences unless I did so, at the same time, I realized I could no longer stay in my present location, hoping quite against logic that she might come back. Having missed luncheon, I needed to return to the Women's Club and partake of dinner. Unlike my brother Sherlock, I could think much more effectively on a full stomach.

Although the news of Lady Cecily's disappearance had, of course, been hushed up by the Alistair family, although the police were discreet, and therefore no word of the escapade had appeared in the press, still: wherever there are servants, there are no secrets. Sir Eustace kept a great many servants; consequently, the dinner-table conversation at the Women's Club bubbled like a babbling brook with secondhand rumour and speculation, most of it having been laughably embroidered in the process of transmission: Lady Cecily Alistair had eloped with a star-crossed secret lover; she had knotted her bedsheets together and lowered herself into his waiting arms, so it was being said. Or, at the opposite extreme, she had shaved her head and gone off to join a nunnery. Or she had leapt from the roof in a desperate attempt to end her hair-shorn, lovelorn life, but had landed, appropriately and harmlessly, in a willow, the symbol of sorrow. Or she had rebelliously fled from parental restraints, aided by an accomplice with a ladder, or, most absurdly, a bow and arrow and a rope.

As I was by far the most junior member of the Women's Club, I seldom spoke very much at table, but I could not let that pass. "Ludicrous," I declared. "How could anyone expect to accomplish such a feat with a bow and arrow?"

Heads nodded, laughter rippled, and someone said, "I find it singularly difficult simply to hit a target."

"So did Sir Eustace himself, when he was young," said Lady Vienna Steadwell. "On one occasion, he missed so widely that he hit one of his sisters in the posterior. Truly," she assured the incredulous. "A surgeon had to be called to remove the arrow, and the whole matter most sternly hushed."

"Well," said one of her friends, "that sounds like the sort of thing Eustace *would* do."

"He exemplifies the consummate masculine blend of incompetence and overconfidence," said another. Laughter followed, but also commiseration for Sir Eustace's wife, Lady Theodora.

Then the table-talk veered off to women's rights and how best to attain them. I spoke no more and listened only a little, for my thoughts were sadly preoccupied with the plight of Lady Theodora and Cecily. It was indeed a tragedy that they were so desperately at the mercy of such a boor as Sir Eustace. Lady Theodora had up until recently entertained the most ambitious plans for Cecily, aspiring to have her presented to the queen. Now, I hoped and dreamed, she might instead plan to take her daughter to Austria to consult with an alienist in order to help the girl reconcile her double personality—of which she had not even been aware until I had deduced it from her journals, so strangely written from right to left in mirror image—

Mirror image!

Although dessert had yet to be served, I leapt up from my place at the dinner table, throwing down my napkin and exclaiming, "What a blind beetle I am!" as I bolted towards my chamber.

Necessarily, coming home from Dr. Ragostin's office I had worn my matronly grey costume, creeping up the back stairs of the Women's Club so as not to be observed by its members before changing into something more fashionable. Now, banging into my bedroom and turning up the gaslight, I seized the ghastly grey suit from where I had flung it on my bed and attacked it, wresting its pockets inside out until at last, huffing with anxiety, I found Cecily's message.

With this precious paper and a hand mirror from my dresser, I sat at the writing table and, approximating the latter to the former, I copied onto a sheet of foolscap Cecily's cipher in mirror image, thus

Then, once again scrawling the key:

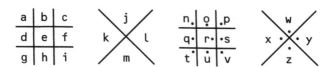

With a tingle of success mingled with a dread of failure, I started to decode.

E . . . O . . . O? Although once more beginning to despair, I persevered. EOOL A I TOOK

Eureka! EOOL A should have been Enola! In her haste, Cecily had made some mistakes in cryptography and spacing, but ENOLA I TOOK made sense and so did what followed. She took MONEY WILL BE SAFE DO NOT WORRY.

She had taken money, she promised she would be safe, and she exhorted me not to worry.

Leaning back in my chair, I took several deep breaths and tried, as Cecily had said, not to worry. Yet, argued my relentless mind, how could I not worry? Cecily could not have gleaned more than a few shillings and pence by searching the pockets of the clothing in my secret room. And—I thought of the cutthroat who had attacked me, the garroter who had tried to kill me—London was *not* safe. Even worse, what if Cecily forgot to be the plucky, resourceful left-handed lady, but became the meek and timid right-handed soul her parents had raised? What might happen to her in that case?

I was the only one who understood the nature and extent of her peril. I *had* to find her. I simply had to.

But how?

Chapter the Eighth

By the next morning, I still had no plan. In such a case, I suppose, my brother Sherlock would have puffed three pipes full of shag tobacco whilst staring into a choking smoky fog of his own making. With unkind thoughts for him and his brilliant deductive powers, I fled my room; I could not bear to stay in there a moment longer. But which way to turn—meaning quite literally upstairs, downstairs, left, or right? Unready to face the outdoors, I wandered the Professional Women's Club until I happened to enter the writing room and was seized by a happier impulse. Sitting down, I appropriated paper and pencils in order to draw.

When I am wrought—which I was—I turn to caricature rather than tobacco, and often some good comes of it. First, I sketched Sir Eustace bellowing and shaking his stick, then with his pursy face all screwed up as if he had just eaten a lemon, then with lifts in his shoes and his hand tucked into his shirtfront, Napoleonic. I included Lady Theodora, richly dressed and tragically beautiful, standing beside him and looming above him to show how ugly and squat he was. On another sheet of paper, I drew, more carefully, Cecily's lovely head, giving her hair its former glory. Then I drew her in a boater and rationals riding a bicycle, then full length in a fashionable dress and hat, smiling, then full length again, but this time huddled in a shawl—

"My goodness, you are talented!" said a voice above my right shoulder, startling me, but not too badly, for I no longer needed to conceal myself from anyone. I looked up to see Lady Vienna beaming at my pictures. "That is Sir Eustace Alistair! Naughty girl, you have captured him like an insect on a pin!" This was the first time in my life, I think, that I had been called naughty in a playful way; she sounded quite delighted. "And is that his wife standing next to him?"

"Lady Theodora, yes. I haven't done justice to her beauty."

"Then she must be beautiful, indeed. And these others?"

"Lady Cecily."

"The daughter who has gone missing?"

"Yes."

"And this girl in the shawl?"

"The very same, and I am filled with foreboding about her."

Those words would not have slipped out so easily, I think and hope, to another listener. Already I felt quite a high regard for Lady Vienna. Seldom does one meet such a woman, in whom amiability is combined with celerity of mind and a high degree of circumspection.

"Shall we discuss it privately over a cup of tea?" she asked me.

"In utmost confidence?" I appealed.

"Of course. Discretion is my middle name."

"Then, by all means." I gathered my papers and stood to accompany her. I know of no scientific basis for the beneficial powers of tea. Nevertheless, while sipping the soothing beverage in a secluded corner of the morning room, gently touched by sunlight and by Lady Vienna's benevolence, I blurted out, "Lady Cecily is left-handed, and being so is at the heart of all her difficulties."

Lady Vienna raised enigmatic eyebrows.

I asked, "What if you had been born left-handed, Lady Vienna?"

"I was, actually," she said softly, "and, by the authority of almighty society, my left hand was declared the mark of the devil, was tied behind me, and I was most sternly ordered not to use it." Seeing my astonishment, she then smiled and asked, "How did you think I became such a thoroughgoing rebel, Enola?"

"But you use your right hand now!"

"My left hand was conquered and defeated. But the long, sad struggle made me hard-minded and stubborn and determined to change this cruel world. Is something similar happening to Lady Cecily?"

I smiled. "Her left hand is not yet conquered and defeated, and it gives her the potential to become much like you. But there are complications." I explained as best I could about the uneasy compromise of Cecily's selfhood. "Her strength has become her weakness," I said in conclusion. "Her left-handed self is quite anyone's equal for confidence and enterprise. But the constant pressure placed upon her to be a sweet and docile right-handed daughter has split her in two. Sometimes she cannot remember where she has been or what she has done. I really think she is a dual personality."

Listening with every sign of deep thought, Lady Vienna probably wondered how I knew all this, but she asked only, "Like Dr. Jekyll and Mr. Hyde?"

"If Mr. Hyde were strong and Dr. Jekyll were weak, yes. And a weak female is in danger on the London streets. I must find her."

"Yes, you intend to be a Perditorian, a finder of the lost," Lady Vienna ruminated aloud, her gaze on her empty cup as if she meant to tell a fortune from her tea leaves. But then she looked at me in much the same way. "But how will you do so?"

With greatest reluctance I admitted, "I have no idea."

But Lady Vienna swooped straight on to another thought. "And even if you succeed, what is to become of the young lady? Legally, she must be returned to the callous care of her father, Sir Eustace. She will not be free of him until she is twenty-one."

And she was now seventeen. Four more years. Ye gods.

"Mercy only knows how many policemen are searching for her," added Lady Vienna.

Not to speak of Sherlock Holmes. As, indeed, I did not speak of him, for I had not yet told Lady Vienna of my mother's demise, and therefore I did not want Lady Vienna to think of anyone named "Holmes." Instead, I stood up and thanked Lady Vienna for tea and sympathy. I was going out. Seldom had I felt more stupid and fuddled, but I hoped walking might clear my mind.

I chose the errand of taking the unfashionable grey gown back to its customary hiding place in "Dr. Ragostin's" secret room, and, after emerging from the underground railway, I did indeed walk the rest of the way there. The big square box of a Georgian brick home stood in a delightfully Bohemian neighbourhood where, in the summertime, gardens flaunted sunflowers, the symbol of Aestheticism, instead of respectable English roses. Sunflowers were yellow, you see, a shocking hue fit to curdle the sensitivities of conservative souls who clothed themselves and their houses in olive, russet, and buff.

Shocking, also, were many of the picturesque persons one might see promenading here: young ladies in canary yellow or vivid Indian-print gowns that flowed loose and airy rather than resembling upholstery of the personage, or long-haired young men wearing velvet knee breeches, white stockings, and patent leather pumps in imitation of Oscar Wilde. Today's being an unusually fine, warm day for October, I noticed many folk out and about: a fashionably dressed femme who minced along in a "bell" skirt that hobbled her at the knees while an enormous yellow ribbon formed a huge bow on her bosom, its streamers trailing almost to the ground; a nanny in a posy-print dress shepherding little children dressed like Kate Greenaway picture-book illustrations; a flower-girl with exceedingly yellow nosegays in a basket. (Peddlers, although not beggars or dancing bears, were tolerated on this iconoclastic and only semi-respectable street.) A man with a pole over his shoulders toted malodourous scrap meat meant for pet dogs and cats. A scissors-sharpener trundled his grinding wheel. A milkman made his rounds. And a tall, stooped greybeard tottered from door to door with a bundle of tools and umbrellas under one arm; he was a "mush-faker," a title not nearly as insulting as it sounds. Skilled craftsmen, "fakers" could fashion almost anything from scraps. The mush-faker could not only mend broken umbrellas, but also put together serviceable "mushrooms" from the ruins of old ones.

I exchanged smiles and nods with most denizens of the street, but the mush-faker busied himself with his back to me as I let myself into "Dr. Ragostin's" premises.

"Miss 'Olmes!" Joddy greeted me with undisguised astonishment. "Two days in a row!"

"Just for a moment, Joddy. You may report back to Mrs. Fitzsimmons." Now that the building functioned primarily as a boardinghouse, Joddy's rather easy employment consisted of running errands for the housekeeper, the cook, and the lodgers.

Once the pesky boy had vanished, I turned the key in the door of the inner sanctum—

And at once forgot all about returning the grey dress to the secret room, for lying crisp and white upon the davenport, where I could scarcely fail to see it, was a sheet of paper unmistakably bearing a message to me. Unceremoniously dropping everything in my arms onto the Turkey carpet, I lunged to seize the paper and look:

Cecily, Cecily; it had to be from Cecily! She knew where the secret door was, she had seen how I had pressed a certain curlicue on the house's wooden moulding to unlatch it, and she had let herself in that way to leave me this message!

So one side of my mind shrieked while the other side chided, *Don't jump to conclusions.* It was my overly civilized rational self that made me try deciphering the note in the conventional way first:

MOOR ETCH IGWCUOG

"There!" my more impulsive self triumphed aloud. "I knew it was mirror image!" Other than a hand mirror in the secret room, the only mirrors available to me in that office were the pier glasses mounted on the walls between bookcases, behind gas fixtures so as to augment the light. Even to use those, I needed three hands: one to hold the message to the mirror, a second to hold a notepad for me to write upon, and a third to wield a pencil. Somehow, I managed, but I felt quite cross by the time I had copied the missive in reverse, and even more vexed as, once more sitting at the desk, I started to decode it.

IOUA

What on earth? It made no sense this way, either!

Persevere, Enola.

IOUAWIG

Wig?

Wig! Jumping up, I hurried across the office, made entry to the secret room, lighted a candle, and looked around. Yes, indeed, one of my best wigs was missing. This would not inconvenience me in the least, as I no longer faced futile struggles with my own hair; at the Professional Women's Club there were maids to help me pile the intractable tresses atop my head. How very intelligent of Cecily to cover her tell-tale shorn head with a wig rather than a shawl! I hoped she might also have found a few more clothes for herself.

Returning to IOUAWIG ("I owe you a wig." How simple after all), I continued to decode her cipher as follows:

HAVE ROOM MUST GET JOB MANY THANKS
You're quite welcome, Cecily!

Leaning back in "Dr. Ragostin's" costly leather chair, I felt a nearly maternal pride in Cecily. No doubt she had taken a different name, as I had done, and she was playing the role of a young working woman, as I had done, and she would establish her independence—

As I had? Balderdash! I should know by now that Cecily was not my twin and could not reasonably be expected to do as I would! At any time, some random circumstance could make her become right-handed, witless, useless, and ornamental.

What might happen to her then?

Like an umbrella torn inside out by the wind, my pride snapped and blew away, replaced by consternation. If persons other than myself discovered that Cecily had two distinct personalities, she stood in great danger of being consigned to a lunatic asylum! A fate perhaps even worse than being caught and returned to her despotic father, Sir Eustace!

Chapter the Ninth

Such were my dismaying thoughts as I returned the grey costume to its hanger, secured the secret room, tidied everything, and, with Cecily's new message tucked into my moss-green merino bosom embroidered with a sunflower motif, I exited the office.

Planning to go home, I rang for Joddy to bring me my hat, gloves, day-cloak, and parasol, but the boy failed to appear. After waiting a few minutes, I frowned, opened the front door of the house, and had a look around for him.

The October day remained unusually warm and sunny. When I had come in, I remembered, the mush-faker had been making his way up my side of the street door-to-door. Now, I noticed he had found a job of work in the house just beyond mine, for he was setting up his tiny folding stool on the pavement preparatory to plying his trade. Like others of his ilk, such as knife-grinders and chair-peggers, he worked outside so as to attract the interest and business of the neighbours. Many such craftsmen become half showman, and knowing this, already a few curious souls loitered to watch.

Including, annoyingly, my boy-of-all-work.

"Joddy!" I called imperiously, and as the scamp came running back to the house where he belonged, the mush-faker glanced up at me with piercing grey eyes.

"Yes, Miss 'Olmes?" inquired Joddy, meek as a sheep, knowing he deserved a scolding for straying from his duties.

But he was spared, for suddenly I had questions to ask him. "Joddy, did that mush-faker knock here, at our door?"

"No, miss."

The evidence of my own ears affirmed this. Occupying the office, I would have heard if anyone had knocked.

Which meant that the mush-faker had skipped right past my very promising house where numerous boarders might well have umbrellas to mend. Why ever had he done so, going on to the next residence?

A patently ludicrous supposition occurred to me, and I attempted to dismiss it. To act upon it in any way would make a public spectacle of me, and potentially a figure of ridicule. Propriety simply forbade—

Hogwash, Enola. You are dithering.

Yes. Yes, I was. Therefore, I needed to lift my chin, stiffen my spine, and march over there—

But wait. Would it not be a great deal more fun if I wore a simpering smile, metaphorically twirled my missing parasol, and soodled into the fray?

I did so, advancing with great girlish finesse before the daring impulse could take leave of me, ambulating right up to the mush-faker to watch him replacing the umbrella's broken old ribs with new ones. The job required considerable strength of hand to force the springy sticks of metal into place. Struggling with them, the greybeard did not look up at me, but said in ill-tempered Cockney, "Aven't yer nuthin' better ter do?"

The other onlookers backed off and wandered away, each making some show of indifference. But I stayed where I was, within arm's reach of the mush-faker. The umbrella ribs did not seem to be cooperating with him, which explained, although did not excuse, his rudeness. But on the other hand, did he not seem a trifle inept? And it occurred to me that his long, grey beard and hair rather got in his way, so why had he not cut them? And why did the porkpie hat perched atop his venerable head never shift position or fall off, no matter how the rigours of his task caused him to exert himself?

I waited until he was finished with the last of eight very annoying umbrella ribs before I spoke.

"If you did that every day of your life," I said, "you would possess some well-developed calluses, but as it is, your hands are visibly red and blistering. I believe one of your fingertips is actually bleeding, Sherlock."

My brother was still laughing in that hearty, soundless way of his as I invited him to come in and take some refreshment. He assented, and once inside the premises that were now becoming familiar to him, he doffed his wig (to which his porkpie hat was attached, as I had thought) and his chin-whiskers, handing them to Joddy just as if they were his usual topper, stick, and gloves.

I told the very startled boy, "Please bring us some lemonade and vanilla wafers or whatever Mrs. Bailey can spare, Joddy." He vanished without a word as Sherlock and I settled into comfortable armchairs facing each other.

I ventured, "You hoped to find Lady Cecily by keeping an eye on me?"

"It seemed not improbable." A true sportsman, he remained gracious in defeat. Making the best of the situation.

A most unexpected situation, having my formidable brother at a disadvantage, however slight. With scarcely an instant's thought I resolved to make the most of my opportunity, for Cecily's sake.

I leaned towards him, facing him eye to eye, as much unlike a blushing, simpering, fluttering maiden as possible. "Sherlock, I would like to ask you a few questions, and if you answer them candidly, I will then answer yours in likewise."

His eyebrows elevated. "You wish to speak to me man to man, as it were?"

"As it were and as it should be."

"I am entirely at your service." He neither smiled nor frowned, but laid back in his chair, put his fingertips together, and closed his eyes. Odd, but I understood from Dr. Watson's accounts of him that this was his deportment when giving a case his full attention.

"Last year, when Mycroft wanted to send me to boarding school," I said, "he told me that he held complete charge over me and he could lock me in my room or take any necessary measures to make me obey him. Do you agree?"

Sherlock said without opening his eyes, "Legally speaking, Mycroft is correct."

"But do *you* agree? Would you, yourself, take such measures?"

He opened his eyes to say, a bit reluctantly, "No. There are times, I admit, when the law is at fault."

"And is that why you act as an independent agent

rather than taking the oath of Scotland Yard? So that you are under no official obligation to enforce the law?"

No longer lounging or drowsing, he sat bolt upright. "Enola!"

"Man to man," I reminded him.

"But you are *not* a man. How could you guess?"

"I will take that as a yes. Now let me ask you another question: Do you feel obliged to take on every problem that is brought before you?"

"Of course not. I reject any case that lacks features of interest or fails to challenge my singular deductive powers."

Such as cases of missing persons. I knew he did not generally bother with them. But I did not say so, not yet.

"And sometimes," Sherlock went on in no worse than his usual lecturing tone, "I find myself out of sympathy with the prospective client. There are persons whose problems are better left unsolved."

Thus we reached my ultimate question. "Then why on earth did you agree to help Sir Eustace locate Lady Cecily Alistair?"

His eyebrows plunged into a V, indicating that I might have pressed him a bit too far, but, happily for me, Joddy ran back into the room at that moment. "Mrs. Bailey wants to know is cold milk and ginger snaps satisfactory, Miss 'Olmes," he blurted as if he might forget the message if he waited for me to turn to him.

"Heavens," I said, for milk and cookies were children's nursery fare, but Sherlock chuckled. I looked at him.

He told Joddy, "Perfectly satisfactory, my boy," and waved him away. "I haven't had such a treat since I wore short pants," he remarked to me.

"How jolly. Sherlock, I must tell you something before we are distracted again. That night when I went to the Alistair house with a bow and arrows and a rope—"

"Aha!" he crowed with cockfight posture. "I knew it had to be you!"

"Do kindly listen, or you cannot have your milk and cookies. That night, my reason for attempting to run a rope up to Lady Cecily's window was so that I could climb it and ask her whether all was well. My dear brother, please bear in mind that the lady is not even remotely the tomboy I am. Therefore, I never in my wildest fancies thought she would herself descend the rope, far less barefoot, in her nightgown—"

"Barefoot?" he interrupted.

"—and with great dispatch."

"In her nightgown?"

"These details were not divulged to you? From your face I can see that they were not. Did no one tell you that Lady Cecily had been locked in her room with all of her clothing and, indeed, all of her personal possessions withheld from her?"

Sherlock parried, or prevaricated, by saying, "I believe it is my turn to ask the questions."

I thought of lying back, steepling my hands, and closing my eyes, but I did not quite dare. Nor did I mimic, "I am entirely at your service." I simply nodded.

He demanded, "What did you do next?"

"I managed to convey Lady Cecily here, partly by carrying her upon my back. I will spare you further details."

"I do not wish to be spared."

"Spared you shall be, nevertheless. I will add only that, the next morning, when you came calling, Cecily was in there—" I tilted my head towards the office.

"—sitting on the davenport, soaking her feet, which were injured from stones." Actually, she had been lying down, but I chose to fib for the sake of modesty and pathos.

I expected no surprise from my brother, and, indeed, he showed none. The gentle reader will kindly understand that I had plans in mind as I divulged such information, but, before I could continue, Joddy came in with a tray of milk and gingersnaps.

Gingersnaps are always served with milk for a reason. "Please feel free to dunk," I told my brother as I took a cookie and dipped it in my milk in order to mitigate its "snap" sufficiently so that I could eat it.

Doing so, he remarked, "Enola, dealing with you seems often to demand a singular lack of decorum."

Decorum being the last thing on my mind, I proceeded with my agenda. "If you are to help Lady Cecily, there is something of greatest importance you ought to know about her. I will give you an example. When fleeing her home with me, she showed the fullest presence of mind and fixity of purpose. But a few hours later, in this house, without any warning she became utterly vapid and helpless. These two extremes of behaviour have also been my experience of her previously." I did not attempt to explain to him that Lady Cecily was left-handed or how being forced to use her right hand had affected her, for I knew my brother possessed only a very limited understanding of such matters. Instead, I stated the case baldly. "Lady Cecily is afflicted with a dual personality, Sherlock."

"Nonsense," he responded without giving even a moment's thought to what I had said. "Do not all women react with such unpredictability?"

"One would think an apostle of logic such as yourself would be ashamed to make such an egregious generalization. Could the case be, rather, that you fail to *understand* women?"

"Argumentum ad hominem."

I rolled my eyes. "Lady Cecily reacts very differently than most people, whether female or otherwise, so much so that when you entered that room, I . . . I knew our voices had given her ample warning, so I hoped she had hidden in the secret room, but I quite feared you would find her still perched stupidly on the davenport."

Although still devouring gingersnaps with apparent

relish, my brother frowned. "Where *was* she? Or more to the point, where *is* she?"

"I do not know. She dressed in some of my clothing and went out the secret door—"

"Secret *door?*"

"She must have done, as there is no other egress from that room."

"*What* secret door? Where?"

Irrelevant, impertinent, annoying questions; I waved them aside. "*Where,* you should be asking, is Lady Cecily? Because where she ventured after leaving here, I simply do not know. Sherlock, I fear for her safety, and I would like to join forces with you to find her, under one condition: we must not, cannot, and I will not return her to her despotic father."

My brother set down his glass of milk so hard that it splashed. "Preposterous! Enola, such a notion is ludicrous to the point of anarchy. How can you expect me—"

But he was interrupted by quite an authoritative knock on the front door.

Chapter the Tenth

"Who on earth?" I wondered aloud, and then we both sat silently attentive as Joddy ran to open the door.

"Message for Miss Enola Holmes," said a phlegmatic male voice.

At once I called, "Here!" and a uniformed commissionaire walked in, tucking his military-style hat under his arm. He handed me a folded paper addressed to me in small, upright, very round penmanship that I recognized with consternation: Cecily's right-handed calligraphy.

Quite presumptuously, considering that he was a guest in my house, Sherlock demanded of the messenger, "Is the young lady waiting for an answer?" If so, I am sure he meant to go seize her.

The commissionaire gave him the blank eye and very properly addressed his reply to me. "Miss Holmes, the sender indicates that she will be in touch." He bowed to me, executed an about-face, and departed.

"If you will wait just a moment," I told Sherlock as I stood up to go stand by one of the windows, presumably for better light but actually to read the message in privacy. It said:

My dearest Enola,

I have heard rumours that my mother has collapsed with brain fever and lies close to death. I am sure you understand I find myself quite frenzied with solicitude for her, yet stricken with doubt; could such ill tidings have been put forth as a scheme to entrap me? Could you please ascertain the truth of the matter?

Eternally in your debt,

Cecily

"What's the matter?" Sherlock demanded. I suppose I looked a bit stricken with doubt myself.

Or frenzied. "Sherlock," I demanded in heightened tones, "when is the last time you saw Lady Theodora?"

"I have not seen her at all, only received a note from her begging me to bring her daughter back to her once again." He must have seen an involuntary flexion of my eyebrows, because he went on with some warmth, "It is entirely your doing, Enola, that I took Cecily home on previous occasions, causing Lady Theodora to credit me with saintly powers. Even though I have on hand a matter of the utmost moment involving the crowned heads of Europe, an impoverished divorcée, and a pink circus poodle, still I could not disregard Lady Theodora's plea."

"But you did not consult with Lady Theodora in person?"

"I was told she was indisposed."

"Yet she sent you a note through the post?"

"No, it was brought to me by a servant."

"A mature and trusted maidservant?"

"Yes." He looked at me oddly. "How did you deduce that?"

"She cannot have gotten it to you in any other way. I think her husband has made her a prisoner just as Cecily was." I crossed the room to him and handed him Cecily's note. "Now we have two problems," I stated as he scanned it. "One: What are Lady Theodora's true circumstances? And two: What are we to do about Cecily, who has most unfortunately transformed from her highly competent left-handed self into a right-handed damsel in distress?"

"What in the name of sanity are you talking about?" Sherlock demanded.

"Sanity is a good name for it. When she is sane, she communicates with me like this." From my bosom I drew

Cecily's most recent missive, and handed it to him.

He glanced at it, saying, "But this is childish. The simplest of . . ." He peered, then evidently he changed his mind when he found he could not immediately decipher it. "What is this?"

"The message of a left-handed lady with the strength of mind to take action, whereas the letter you just read is the dainty and decorative missive of a right-handed girl far too much affected by the dictates of society."

"I do not understand."

"For the present, my dear brother, it is not necessary that you should understand. I have urgent business elsewhere; I must bid you adieu." I crossed to the bell rope and rang, once again, for Joddy to bring me my cloak, gloves, et cetera. "No doubt you wish to remain here in case Lady Cecily appears, or you will have your Baker Street Irregulars watch for her. You are quite welcome to do so." The page boy entered. "Joddy, my things, please."

In heightened tones, Sherlock demanded, "Enola, where are you going?"

"I am going about my business, as I am sure you will go about yours. If you would care to meet, please do not expect to find me here, but a note at my club will reach me. Au revoir."

His mouth opened but no words emerged, and I

acted as if none were likely to. With my ladylike paraphernalia in place, I sailed out the door.

Truth to tell, I could take no action regarding Lady
Theodora until after dark. But I wished to leave Sherlock thinking that I had matters thoroughly under
control. Also, I wished him to believe I was sure
Cecily would not return to Dr. Ragostin's manse;
I needed him to think I had arranged to meet her
elsewhere.

Would that it were so!

I returned to the Women's Club in a most uncertain mood, threw my feminine appurtenances across
the room onto my bed rather than laying them down,
doffed my boots so forcefully that five buttons popped
off, nearly said something unforgivable because I would
have to sew the dratted things back on, thrust my fingers into my hair instead (thus ruining my coif), sat
down with my stocking feet up on an ottoman, and set
about tidying my mind.

I did so by scrawling a list, thus:

Remember that Cecily is not a tomboy like me.

Not able to run as fast as I, or defend herself as well.

Almost certainly not carrying a dagger concealed in her corset.
She is smaller and daintier.

The clothing she appropriated from me is too large for her and will cause her to look make-shift, genteel but poor.

She is seeking gainful employment. Doing what?

Surely, not toiling for sixteen hours a day in a cotton mill or match factory. As a better-class "working girl," she had only a few choices. I felt sure Cecily had never learned typewriting and therefore could not become office help or a print compositor. Telegraph or telephone operator, perhaps, although positions were few and vied for. Clerk in a post office or department store—not possible immediately, for she would need attractive clothes that fit properly! Nanny, governess—the same difficulty about clothes, but even worse, someone who had known her as Sir Eustace's daughter might recognize her.

Her prospects are discouraging. Can she survive independently of her family?

I had managed to do so only because my mother had provided me with so much money.

As a dual personality?

No. Alas, no. I greatly feared that Cecily might end up as a homeless street beggar, a friendless resident in a lunatic asylum, or even worse.

I must find her. Yet how can I possibly return her to Sir Eustace?

Thus put, the situation seemed quite hopeless, but I held my despair at bay.

Enola, think. Logic had solved thornier problems.

Premise: Sir Eustace intended to dispose of his daughter, Lady Cecily, as he saw fit, and he had the legal power to do so.

True or false?

Alas, true.

Was there any way out? If only Lady Cecily did not have such a fragile, split personality; if only she were stronger . . .

Enola, you cannot change her overnight.

O doom, O gloom, O despair, was there no way . . .

Enola, think!

Think think think think . . . I knew I had to approach this problem from an entirely different direction, but what was it?

Stop wishing Cecily were stronger. Instead, think: How to weaken her father?

At once this new concept galvanized me. As if lightning had struck, sitting bolt upright, I grabbed the papers I had been scribbling on, crumpled them, threw them in the trash, and raised a clenched fist.

Carry the fight to the enemy. Yes! Weaken Sir Eustace. Yes!

Yes!!

But—how?

My erect posture wilted, for I had no idea. How, indeed?

I got up and paced around the room several times, trying to achieve a fortified frame of mind. To this end, I essayed some gymnastic exercises, such as chest expansions and lateral tractions of the neck and arms. I jumped in place several times, and, finally, I applied cold water from the washbasin to my face. Then I stood in front of the window peering at the day, which had clouded over and darkened. Confound the weather. Pay no attention. I murmured, "Brain, do your duty."

I was talking aloud, I haplessly mused, to an organ hidden within my own dolichocephalic skull yet said to be grey, like the sky.

"Stuff and nonsense! Think!" I exhorted myself, directing my mind like a telescope towards the matter of Sir Eustace Alistair.

Moments passed, but slowly I found a focus. Surely, I thought, such a boorish baronet with so many visible flaws—meanness, overweening ambition, pusillanimity, mental torpor—surely he must have done things he would quite wish to hide?

Of course.

Perhaps he had cheated at cards or reneged on debts of honour.

Perhaps he had dallied with brazen ladies of the theatre.

Perhaps he footled with servant girls.

He had a bad temper. Perhaps he had at some time *struck* a servant or a woman?

Perhaps he had run wild in his youth. Perhaps he had succumbed to hard liquor or worse. Perhaps he had even been known to frequent opium dens!

Perhaps there was a shameful streak of lunacy in his family, an aunt secreted in an attic somewhere.

Perhaps . . .

And perhaps and perchance and mayhap, indeed, but how to happen upon information thereof?

Hmmm.

———————

"What a lovely frock," Lady Vienna Steadwell greeted me when, complete with a pair of yellow silk house slippers that matched the sunflowers embroidered on my bodice, I sat down facing her in one of the morning room's matronly wicker chairs. "Is it not a grand thing that verticality has at last come into fashion?"

"Yes!" And we laughed together because I had understood her immediately; like her, I was tall, slender, and lacked lateral projections. It was a blessing to both of us that decades of vogue for the wasp-waisted hourglass figure had passed.

"I am myself tempted to try one of those gowns with a graceful gored skirt," she said thoughtfully, "although I have never been one to require the latest in fashion. Or the latest in anything else, for that matter."

"What?" I quipped. "You have never been one to take daily airings in a gilded barouche drawn by a matched pair of dapple greys?"

She reacted with laughter, and we then had a nice catty chat about the foibles of London's social elite, gentlemen in the very most recent imported-from-France style wearing sack coats with only the top button fastened, and ladies with the upper sleeves of their gowns puffing ever larger. My design was to steer the conversation towards Sir Eustace Alistair. If ever he had done anything disreputable and hidden from polite society, it seemed to me that Lady Vienna, with her wise mind and many connexions, might know of it. But it was one thing for me to confide in her my concerns for Cecily and another thing entirely for her to reveal to me secrets about Sir Eustace.

". . . foolish young ladies," she was saying, "who must have the latest thing in Godey's Lady's Book even if their mamas have to go without a month of dinners to pay for them."

"Lady Cecily is not particularly foolish," I protested, "but she is well dressed, and so are her many sisters, and so is her mother. I think Lady Theodora Alistair must be a marvelous manager to be able to keep up such good appearances."

"Appearances. Exactly." With predatory zest, Lady Vienna leaned towards me. "Sir Eustace has always been the most relentless of social climbers, determined to match or exceed every extravagance of his sisters. He and Lady Theodora live far beyond their means, and have always done so."

"But how, then, are they not bankrupt?"

Lady Vienna, finding herself on the verge of committing gossip, leaned back into her capacious wicker chair, primly replying, "I am sure I do not know."

Something in her manner made me feel quite sure she *did* know a great deal. I gave her my most thoughtful regard. "Lady Vienna, I recall a conversation referring to an arrow in the derriere of Viscountess Inglethorpe—or was it Baroness Merganser? And a remark that it was the sort of thing Sir Eustace would do. I quite desire to know what else he has done, but not for idle gossip's sake."

Studying me with an earnestness that matched my own, she asked, "Why, then?"

"To give his daughter and his wife the means to knacker him if he attempts to tyrannize them any longer."

The lady's celadon-green eyes widened. "Do you have knowledge of where Lady Cecily might be?"

I replied only with what I hoped was an enigmatic smile.

Lady Vienna's lovely eyes brightened by the moment as she studied me. Then, leaning close to me and keeping her voice low, she said, "I have heard there are a bow and some arrows missing from the Physical Culture Boudoir's equipment pantry."

Maintaining silence, I shrugged my shoulders.

"I do declare." Lady Vienna's eyes sparkled, and she smiled even though she seemed to attempt not to. "I ought to be terribly shocked." But, at the same time, she relaxed into the cushioned depths of her chair. For several moments, her eyes peered absently as she thought. Then her soft green-grey gaze returned to me. "Very well, dear, I will tell you whatever I can, for you are a young woman after my own heart. But I must caution you: whispers and rumour and hearsay are all I have to offer you, and I do not think they will achieve the desired result. Somehow you must find proof."

With a nod of acknowledgement, I settled myself to listen.

Chapter the Eleventh

And I listened well.

And parted from Lady Vienna with thanks.

After a late luncheon and a quick change of clothing for the sake of becoming inconspicuous (taupe walking suit, standard attire for genteel women on London's streets), I spent the rest of the day out and about, taking a tram to an East End district of used clothing shops and eventually returning with all the disparate piebald parts of a lady's maid's uniform: black dress; white, ruffled apron and collar and cuffs; coarse black stockings;

and clumsy black shoes with huge grosgrain bows. It would have been far easier to buy a new costume entire at a department store, but, in brand-new clothing, I would be spotted as an impostor before I got through the kitchen, whereas I hoped at least to reach the back stairs of the stately Alistair residence. For more than one reason, I needed to pay Lady Theodora a visit.

A maid's uniform renders one piebald, to my way of thinking, because it is all black and white. Or perhaps, I thought as I struggled to get my white apron tied around my black middle with a respectable bow, perhaps I more closely resembled a magpie. Once I had gotten my white collar and cuffs fastened properly onto my black dress, I strove to pin my white cap straight on hair done up meekly in a bun. Piebald, magpie, same root word: pie.

Hmm.

With a simple basket of the sort one carries via its handle over one's arm, I went downstairs to the kitchen, where I filched a pie pan, placed it in my basket, and covered it with a pristine white dish towel from the linen press.

I took a deep breath, called my mother's face to

mind, told myself, *You will do quite well on your own, Enola,* and sallied forth.

Maids do not take cabs; I could have trusted only Harold, my favourite and very discreet cabbie, and my messenger boy had not been able to obtain him. So I was forced to rely on shank's mare. Already it was dark, and while evening zephyrs may have been wafting else-where in England, London simply became windy and cold so that I presently became quite chilled walking all the way to the Alistairs' Mayfair neighbourhood. But, as planned, I arrived before bedtime, during the drowsy evening hour when masters and servants alike begin to yawn and look at the clock. When no one is terribly alert or thinking very clearly. I hoped.

I, myself, felt rather too alert for comfort. Survey-ing the side of the manse, I saw light behind the or-ganza curtains in Lady Theodora's windows—I knew which rooms were hers, having previously visited her boudoir in disguise as "Mrs. Ragostin." While a sto-rey less lofty than Cecily's, Lady Theodora's chambers nevertheless loomed far above me, with neither ivy-clad walls nor drainpipes to make them accessible by climbing.

Moving figures cast vague shadows on the curtains, causing unease in both my mind and my abdominal region because Lady Theodora was not alone. But faint heart ne'er won fair lady, et cetera. Onwards, upwards, Excelsior!

I went around to the kitchen door, which was not yet locked as slops were still being carried out. Just before striding in, I remembered to amend my posture. I slumped, ducked my head, filled my cheeks with air, and schooled my face to look stupid. Then, with the scuttling, cockroach gait of a lifelong drudge accustomed to having things thrown at her, I slipped in.

The cook slumped in the rocking chair beside her stove, head askew, snoring. The scullery maids drooped over the sinks. I had crossed almost to the base of the back stairs before a masculine voice challenged, "You there! What are you doing in here?"

The butler had spotted me from his pantry whilst polishing silver. I bobbed at him, looking as slack and stupid as possible, indeed allowing saliva to trickle from one corner of my mouth. Displaying my basket and gesturing at its contents as if to indicate I was running an errand, like a mouse I scampered upstairs.

"Wait!" the butler called after me. "Where do you think you're going?" I did not, of course, wait; indeed, as silently as possible, I began to run, taking the stairs two at a time. With luck, I could reach Lady Theodora's boudoir door before he sent someone after me (for it was far beneath his dignity to pursue me himself). The most important thing I needed to do was find out Cecily's mother's condition: whether she was deathly sick, as rumoured, or perfectly well.

Ground floor, first storey, second. I burst out of the stairs onto a servant's landing to find myself in a left-handed house, mirror-image to the one I remembered; I had come at everything backwards. Which door was Lady Theodora's?

Enola, THINK.

I remembered myself as Mrs. Ragostin walking up the front stairs, led by the adamantine butler. Turning. Being shown into Lady Theodora's boudoir.

Then I ran to what I hoped was the right door, knocked, tried to turn the knob, found it locked, knocked again.

"Who is it?" a woman's voice, a servant's judging by her accent, called sharply from inside.

In a high-pitched voice, I piped, "Ragostin pie for Lady Alistair!"

"What?" Of course, she had no idea what Ragostin pie was. Nor did I, but it didn't matter. I heard footsteps, heard a key turn, and the door opened a crack, through which a matronly, grey-haired servant peered at me. "How'd yer get up 'ere?"

"Ragostin pie!" I shrilled so that no one within could fail to hear me.

I heard a gasp, then some small object thudding to the carpet, then a gentle voice I knew: Lady Theodora's, crying, "Let her in!"

I also heard footsteps hurrying up the stairs.

Rather than letting me in, the servant at the door turned to protest, "But my lady, what if—"

"Let her in, Phyllis! At once!" But footsteps sounded too close for me to wait any longer. I hurled myself at the narrow opening of the door, widening it with bodily force as I shoved through, necessarily colliding with the servant. She kept both her footing and her head, however, closing the door behind me, locking it, then putting the key in her pocket.

Seated on a dainty Japanese chair that perfectly

framed her own delicate beauty, fully clothed in a lacy tea-frock, her hair done up in ribbons, Lady Theodora stared wide-eyed at me, as I am sure I was staring at her. Although she looked thin and wan, as might be expected after her recent trials, quite apparently she was neither ill nor on her deathbed.

Someone knocked at the door. Raising a finger to her lips, Lady Theodora signaled me to be silent, and once again the loyal Phyllis showed commendable presence of mind. She stepped away from the door, then yawned to ask in a drowsy voice, "Who is it?"

"Jenkins 'ere. You seen anybody wot don't belong in the 'ouse?"

"What on earth?"

"If you seed 'er, you'd know. Never mind."

Phyllis played her part to admiration. "But whatcher talking about?"

"Never mind, I said!" Jenkins could be heard hastening away.

Lady Theodora smiled at her maid, then at me, mischievously, then whispered, "My dear Mrs. Ragostin, what sad circumstances have forced you into domestic service?"

Snatching my absurd white cap off my head and dropping my basket, I crossed the room to her. "Actually, I'm Cecily's friend Enola."

"Ah!" Her exquisite eyes widened. "That explains a great deal." She reached up to me and took my hand in both of hers. "How is Cecily?"

"Most desirous to know how *you* are." Still hand in hands with Lady Theodora, I sat beside her on a chair brought there for me by the maid. "She heard whispers that you were ill."

The lady rolled her brilliant eyes. "A lie of my husband's, by which he hoped to lure Cecily back here. I am sure he has deceived some of the servants. But Phyllis and I deceive *him*." The lady smiled at the matronly servant standing guard over both of us; Phyllis gave back to her a smile as fond as a mother's. "He thinks he has me imprisoned here in my room, quite unaware that there are such things as extra keys."

"Phyllis took a message to my brother for you."

"To Sherlock Holmes? Yes. I was quite frantic at first, Enola, thinking that Cecily had been kidnapped. Now I have come to think she went of her own free will, but still, I want her back quite desperately. Where is she?"

How dreadful that question made me feel, for I did not know! But I bluffed. "She has clothing, money, and a room. I am in contact with her and she with me. Lady Theodora, she cannot possibly come back to you if you continue to allow her father to treat her so heinously."

Lady Theodora stiffened, withdrawing her hands from mine. "Allow? *Allow?*" She tried to laugh; she sounded like shattering glass. "How can I do otherwise? I have attempted to leave him, but having eight children—"

"I know you were forced to return for lack of funds. But I hope to provide you other means of freedom."

"What means, for heaven's sake?"

"Surely, as Sir Eustace's wife, you must know of things he has done, things that would greatly embarrass him were they to reach the public ear?"

For so Lady Vienna Steadwell had told me.

But Lady Theodora's eyes flew wide open, her brows steepled, she jerked upright and rigid like a wrought-iron fence paling, and her hands flew up to cover her gasping mouth; for a moment, I thought that she was going to shriek as if she had seen a rat.

All would be lost if I could not coax this very proper, aristocratic lady past her inbred abhorrence of what, no doubt, she would call blackmail.

"Lady Theodora," I said in my most soothing tone, "what is so dreadful about preventing Sir Eustace from ill-using you or Cecily ever again?"

"But the disgrace would destroy him! And he could go to gaol!"

This confirmed for me that the rumours of which Lady Vienna had told me were true: Sir Eustace had indeed done criminal things with the bodies of his deceased servants.

I responded in my gentlest tone, "Exactly. Therefore, we can force him to be sensible. But, to gather proof, I need the names of his victims—"

"Oh, I couldn't!" She covered her entire face with her hands as if she were going to weep.

This was not going well, not well at all, until an unexpected voice spoke up. "'E's been a bad husband ter ye," said the maid, Phyllis, "and ye deserve better." She turned to me. "The first one were Timothy Burke.

'E was a footman," she said, "and, after that, it were an upstairs maid, Imogen Saunders, and then a groom named Sims."

From my bodice, I snatched paper and pencil to write them down. But, before I could do so, a male voice, unmistakably Sir Eustace's, roared from somewhere not nearly far enough away, "Theodora!"

Her hands flew up to flutter, feeble like dying moths, beside her ashen, pale face.

I sprang up, almost as helpless as she, turning in circles, trying to sight a hiding place. But Phyllis acted at once, shoving my absurd basket behind a mass of potted plants and picking up the cap I had dropped.

Ponderous footsteps sounded nearby. Sir Eustace's voice menaced, "Theodora!" Most unwisely, I reached for my dagger, pulling it from its sheath in the busk of my corset.

But, in a low voice, Phyllis said, "Put that back," and as I did so, she took me by both shoulders from behind, propelling me around a corner. "Hit's a good thing yer skinny as a child. Into the laundry chute with ye."

"Theodora! Answer me!" roared Sir Eustace from directly outside the door. Phyllis let go of me to fling aside a decorative hanging on the wall. Beneath it yawned a dark orifice so unappealing of aspect that I must admit I hesitated.

But I heard Sir Eustace's key rattling in the lock. Phyllis heard it, also, and gave me a hard shove between my shoulder blades. Headfirst, into the unholy hole I went, with Phyllis giving me another shove on the posterior and whispering, "Tuck up yer feet; cross yer hankles; don't make a noise!" Then she must have covered my retreat with the drape that hung on the wall, for I found myself in total darkness and concealment, but not, alas, in safety. Jaws clamped so as not to scream, quite rapidly I slid downwards.

Chapter the Twelfth

"A spy, Theodora! A spy in the house! Who is it?" bellowed Sir Eustace, but those were the last words of his I heard that evening, for the laundry chute took me like a metal dragon and swallowed me. Down that inanimate gullet I shot with a force that stunned me, body and mind. Apparently, I had not previously given sufficient respect to Sir Isaac Newton's musings on natural philosophy. I had, of course, experienced his law of gravity when falling out of trees, but I found it infinitely more puissant and fearsome within the blind confines of the laundry chute. Only breathlessness, I think, kept me from shrieking.

Sliding facedown, I swished around a turning, then another, before I regained sufficient wit to realize several simple facts at once: Other laundry chutes from upstairs fed into this one. It zigzagged to accommodate them. I could slow my pell-mell descent by clinging to them with my hands, but, for Lady Theodora's sake, I must not let anyone hear me. I must not release the scream caught in my vocal cords or bang the sides of the chute with my shoes.

Using only my arms, therefore, and not my legs or feet, I managed to turn over so that I was sliding, albeit still headfirst, on my back. No sooner had I done so than I felt my shoulders swoop into a zag, or perhaps a zig, and I reached up with both arms, both hands outspread, feeling for—

Yes! Catching hold of the edge of a metal junction, I held on, straining as if I grasped the reins of a team of runaway horses, and managed to pull my hurtling personage to a halt.

For some moments, I simply clung there, breathing deeply in relief from dizzying speed, in thanks for even such tenuous control of my situation, in joyous emancipation from the tyranny of gravity. Even total darkness seemed far less fearsome when one could lie still in it.

Rather than hurtling downwards any longer, might I now climb up the secondary chute, emerge into someone's bedroom after he or she was asleep, creep out with all due caution, and make my escape from the Alistair household on my own two clever feet?

This plan seemed far preferable to being dumped on my head at some unknown destination.

I put it into action at once. Pulling myself to a sitting position as silently as I possibly could, careful not to bang anything with any part of my personage, I explored the opening of the other chute with my hands, then poked myself into it by careful degrees—once I had gotten my shoulders and torso in, how good it felt to stand on my feet once again!—and by pressing against the sides of it with opposing portions of my anatomy, I began to climb like a chimney sweep, rejoicing mentally: *This is much better.*

And so it was, until the chute narrowed. Blinder than a mole in a tunnel at nighttime, I could not possibly foresee this calamity, but suddenly there I was, wedged in by my shoulders on both sides. I attempted various slithering and wriggling manoeuvres that only made matters worse until I became stuck like a cork in a wine bottle. My terrified heart pounded so hard one would think it might shake me loose, but no. My narrower parts were trapped (head) and held immobile (shoulders), while from the waist down my hands, feet, and skirt swung free as a bell but ineffectual.

I envisioned myself starving to death in the obscurity of that laundry chute, my mummified remains undiscovered for generations of Alistairs.

Nonsense, Enola. Their laundry would gather atop you, causing them to investigate the blockage.

But this reasoning did not help. I felt horribly afraid, quite cold with fright. Really, might it not be time to cry out for help? Truly, if I were discovered, what could Sir Eustace do to me?

What he did to others.

"Oh, help," I whispered, but then I seemed to hear my mother's voice speaking inside my head, *Enola, you will do quite well on your own. Think.*

So I thought, ideas tinged with hysteria. Could I slither out of my piebald uniform like a snake shedding its skin to escape, indecent but free, leaving my unlovely clothing behind? Unlovely and uncomfortable, with its starched collar rasping my neck, cuffs scratching my wrists, apron galling my back with its knotted bow . . . I could at the very least get rid of the apron!

So, more idiotically than brilliantly, I began struggling to untie the bow. My hands, hanging below my immobilized shoulders, could not reach it, so I grasped the waistband and turned the apron backwards, with the bow in front. Struggling with the knot I could not see, I untied it, then held one loose end in each hand while the apron itself hung almost at my feet—my poor, dangling feet. Bending my knees, I lifted my feet to place them, with much fumbling, on the waistband of the apron. With no notion of pulling myself up by my bootstraps or down by my apron strings, I put my feet there just because I thought they might feel better with a place to rest, although their weight strained my arms downwards—

And freed me, greatly to my surprise and consternation as I found myself plummeting downwards in utter darkness. With a gasp like a sort of inverted scream, I dropped the apron and braced my elbows and knees against the sides of my metal prison, attempting, without much success, to slow my fall. My cumbersome shoes made a considerable bang as I regained the larger laundry chute from which I had originated. Quite involuntarily, I sat down, then lay down atop my apron, once more sliding on my back like a benighted toboggan down a metal slope—but, all the fates be praised, not headlong anymore! Now, wherever I was going, my feet would arrive first.

Almost before I decided to resign myself to this fate, I met it. I felt the laundry chute hurtle me into a steep descent, steeper, almost perpendicular, then—nothing. Wildly thinking that I would expand and explode if I did not scream, I fell through blank black air—for a mercifully brief period of time. I landed, safely and blessedly unhurt, in something soft and springy. It felt, and distinctly smelled, like dirty laundry. Disgusting. Yet I must admit that, for a grateful moment, I simply lay in my nest of malodourous cloth.

And I would have done so for several moments more, if it were not that I heard a door open and saw a shaft of light—it seemed piercingly bright after so much darkness—coming from upstairs. The cellar stairs. Sitting up to gawk around me, I saw enough to realize I was in the cellar, peering over the edge of a sizeable laundry bin.

"Sounded like a boiler blowing, so it did," said a man's voice, and I heard the footsteps of more than one person start to descend.

Instantly, I ducked my head, and, as silently as possible, I burrowed into the pile of dirty laundry, making sure to cover as much of me as I could, but especially my feet, hands, and face, despite the fact that soiled unmentionables made me wrinkle my nose. My black skirt stuck out a bit, but that didn't matter; it was laundry, was it not? I lay stock-still.

"The water heater don't seem like it's been up to any mischief," said another man. To inspect it, he must have been carrying a lantern or a candle, but, once again blind to my environs, I had no idea which.

"I suspect a washerwoman left the lid open on the washing machine, and it simply fell down," said a supercilious voice, unmistakably that of the butler. "Or a flatiron rattled on the stove or something of the sort."

"All by itself?" said the first voice, probably that of a footman. "What if that sneaking girl you saw earlier is down here?"

"And what if she's been taken care of?" The butler sounded chilly. "Those who wish to keep their places with Sir Eustace Alistair do not question odd sounds too closely. Come along. I, for one, have my work yet to finish."

The other two must have assented, for I heard all three trudging back up the stairs, and I heard the door close behind them.

When, a few moments later, I surfaced from my concealing sea of laundry, I faced darkness again—darkness rendered fearsome by what the butler had said. Taken care of? I had no desire to be "taken care of" in any way Sir Eustace might arrange for me.

My white apron and cap were already gone; I rid myself of my white collar and cuffs, thus making myself almost as uniformly black as the night. I considered shedding my awkward, heavy shoes but decided I would need them in case I had to run; going forth in stocking feet would deplorably slow me down. So then, with stealth and trepidation, I clambered out of the laundry bin to stand on the plank floor, looking around blindly—no, not quite blindly! A faint blush of light glowed out from around the fire-bed doors of several cast-iron stoves no doubt dedicated to the heating of flatirons. In the gloom, I made out the dim forms of ironing boards, coal scuttles, washstands, a wringer, baskets of clean linens that had been sprinkled and rolled like soggy logs of cloth to await pressing, and—most interestingly—the washing machine. Never having seen one of those before, I stole towards it—blast my clumsy footwear!—to inspect it. My curiosity was quickly satisfied. The modern device was nothing more than a wooden tub with paddles on a shaft that ran up through the lid and a crank on top by which to turn them. This could not have been an easy task. Washerwomen, I surmised, developed the strength of oxen.

Unless I desired to make the acquaintance of washerwomen or cooks in the morning, I quite needed to get out of that cellar.

Light showed around the door at the top of the stairway; I could not go up there, where the butler was probably still counting the spoons. A bit more light, the faint, foggy light of the London night, showed through very small windows set high on the walls, too high for me to reach even by climbing on hot stoves, hardly a wise procedure in any case. My heart began to beat rather hard, like the wings of a blackbird frantic to get out of a black cage. The only part of the cellar I had not yet examined was the far corner, which seemed to be partitioned off for some reason.

As silently as I could, setting my feet down softly and being very careful not to blunder into anything, I walked over there, felt my way along plank walls until I found an opening, then looked in—but I could see absolutely nothing. It was as black as Sir Eustace's soul in there.

The thumping of my heart drove me to take desperate measures. Feeling around in a kindling box near one of the stoves, I found a long splinter of wood. Then, trying to be as quiet as possible while not quite succeeding, I lifted a stove lid and thrust my splinter into the hot embers below until it flamed. Withdrawing it, I set the stove lid back in place; cast iron *would* clang against cast iron, no matter how gentle I was. There was no time to waste. Lifting my makeshift torch like a candle, I hastened at a frenzied shuffle to explore the mystery in the corner.

It was a coal bin, of course, with quite a mountain of coal in it leading up to an odd little double door at the top. This aperture had to be for the delivery of coal from a wagon, and it had to lead out to the mews! Or so, with quickened breathing, I hoped.

With happy haste, I clambered up the pile of coal, unfastened the double door (which latched on the inside), and opened it wide.

Yes! I could tell by the smell of fresh, cold air that it led outside—but not quite as simply as I had hoped. I faced a coal chute.

I could climb into it. It was quite large enough to accommodate me.

It was filthy.

My splinter of wood had burned down almost to my fingertips, so I blew it out and stood, eminent upon a coal heap, in darkness. I contemplated the consequences of ascending a coal chute. I sighed. Then I smiled and proceeded.

I am, by habituation if not by nature, a nocturnal creature. So was my brother Sherlock, according to what

I had read in the journals of his friend Dr. Watson. When I emerged, successfully, albeit besmirched all over, from the Alistairs' coal chute, I sensed by the silence of the city around me that the hour must be quite late. But I urgently wanted to speak with Sherlock.

So, as there were no cabs on the streets, I ambulated, clip-clopping like a horse in my unfortunate footwear. But noise no longer mattered; I was free! So, springing with glee, I sprinted, I loped, I *ran* all the way there—with greatest pleasure, because I dearly love to run but cannot do so when anyone is watching, for the foolish reason that well-bred females are supposed to soodle delicately everywhere they go; decency forbid any such woman should stretch her limbs in public! Now, however, there was no one to see me shamelessly enjoying myself as a biped. Or if anyone did see me speeding through the night, with my face—covered with coal dust—nearly as black as my dress, perhaps they thought me a spectre.

After a remarkably brief time, I halted on the pavement in front of 221 Baker Street. Looking up at the bow window of Sherlock's lodgings, I saw his gas light turned up high; he was awake, perhaps performing one of his all-night chemical experiments. His sweet old landlady, Mrs. Hudson, was surely in bed fast asleep. So I did not ring, as I did not want to disturb her, especially as my hobgoblin appearance might cause her to shriek. Instead, I trotted around to the backyard, climbed the plane tree, stepped onto the kitchen's projecting roof, squatted by Sherlock's bedroom window, and rapped smartly upon it.

I heard an exclamation and the sound of shattering glass, as if in sympathy with the window I had assailed. Presently, the bedroom door opened; illumination from the sitting room beyond showed Sherlock in a dressing gown and carrying a candle. Apparently, its flame reflected in the window glass prevented him from seeing me properly, for he demanded, "Who's there?"

"Enola."

He strode over to the window and opened it wide, then stood looking me up and down with only the slightest elevation of his eyebrows. "Thank you for knocking," he said. "Last time you simply let yourself in. Have you been sweeping chimneys?"

"Climbing a coal chute to get out of the Alistair house."

"Of course." He sounded a bit droll.

"I went to speak with Lady Theodora. The rumour regarding her health is a canard. Although heartlessly confined to her boudoir, she is neither languishing nor ill, much less on her deathbed."

"This is hardly news worth my breaking a beaker for."

"There is more. May I come in?"

"Most irregular, Enola! Grimy spectacle that you are? Think of what your coal dust will do to the carpets, the furniture!" But I heard mirth in his voice; after all, this was the man who had decorated his sitting room wall with Queen Victoria's initials done in bullet holes. Standing aside, Sherlock Holmes bowed and extended one arm in a gracious gesture of hospitality, inviting me to enter as if his rear window were his front door.

Chapter the Thirteenth

A quantity of water that had gone cold remained in Sherlock's ewer, allowing me to cleanse my face and hands somewhat, leaving his washstand in deplorable condition. After that, I found a great rumple of discarded newspapers in a corner of his sitting room, and, with them, I covered the upholstery on the only habitable chair in the room before I made use of it. Perching on a stool at the table upon which he had set up his science experiment, Sherlock resembled a large and leggy bird.

Pointing his beak of a nose towards me, he remarked, "With all due rejoicing for the good health of Lady

Theodora, there must be something more to bring you here in this state at this hour."

I shrugged, raising a cloud of coal dust around my shoulders. "I would like to know whether you have yet found Lady Cecily."

"I have every hope of doing so if she ventures anywhere near Dr. Ragostin's house tonight."

It was as I thought; he had his Baker Street Irregulars on the lookout. I quite expected he would find Lady Cecily, perhaps even tonight, and this was the reason I had not waited until morning to call upon him. I needed to convince him not to return Lady Cecily to her home-cum-prison, or at least not straightaway.

"Sherlock," I asked, "do you agree with me that Sir Eustace Alistair is the worst sort of bully, a domestic tyrant?"

"I dare say. But, Enola, the law—"

The law gave the domestic tyrant ownership of his daughter, as if she were a mynah bird. I interrupted, "I have reason to believe Sir Eustace is also a scoundrel, a heartless villain, and perhaps even a criminal."

Although my brilliant brother did not recline, steeple his fingers, and close his eyes, I could see I had captured his attention.

"He aspires above his station," I went on, "and overspends to the point of financial ruin, which he has fended off for years only by selling the bodies of his deceased servants to dissecting rooms, and sometimes their teeth for dentures, or their hair for wigs."

"Indeed," Sherlock murmured, half-lidding his eyes as if he were growing sleepy. But, below the lids, his grey eyes glinted like knife blades. Or should I say, like surgeon's scalpels? It was medical students who craved more corpses than the prisons could provide for them and who paid well for extra (albeit shorn and/or toothless) specimens, no questions asked, knowing quite well that the bodies they dissected might have been murdered by a specialized method that left no marks, a crime known as "burking."

The gentle reader must understand what a scandal Sir Eustace's disposal of his servants was, even if they died of natural causes. By custom, they should have been given decent burial. Even setting aside religious strictures regarding resurrection of the body, to involuntarily donate one's hair, teeth, or personage, to have one's anatomy bared to the scrutiny of strangers, then sliced open—just the thought made me shudder.

Sherlock cut me a sharp—oh, dear, runaway metaphors must be curbed. He looked at me impatiently, I mean, saying, "Data, Enola, data! I cannot build a case without data."

"I have the names of three victims," I announced, trying to recall them. "Phyllis told them to me," I said to stall for time whilst realizing, with a sick and sinking feeling, that my mind seemed to have dropped the names somewhere in the laundry chute. "Phyllis is the name of the maid who brought you Lady Theodora's message."

"And the names of the three victims?" said Sherlock with some asperity.

"They will come to me."

"Enola, you cannot accuse Sir Eustace of burking without evidence!"

"I have not accused him of burking. I only said—Burke!" I would venture that never has a girl filthy with coal dust and sitting upon newspapers in the wee hours felt more happily relieved. "The first victim was Timothy Burke, a footman. I imagine he died a natural death; the questionable aspect is how Sir Eustace disposed of the body. Then there was an upstairs maid named Imogen Saunders." Once I had recalled one name, the others came back to me. "And a groom named Sims. I believe Phyllis would have told me more, but, at that point, Sir Eustace impended, and I was obliged to exit by way of the laundry chute."

"By Jove," said Sherlock, mimicking the hearty bluster of a squire who has been hunting pheasant, "we had splendid chuting today, so we did, just splendid."

"Quite," I agreed, as straight-faced as he. "I hope not in vain," I added. "Sherlock, have I managed at all to influence you regarding Lady Cecily's fate should you find her?"

He stiffened. "I make it a practice not to be influenced."

"Then perhaps 'influence' is the wrong word. I ask you only to apply logic. The lady's father is inclined to ill-treat her. Returning to him, should she not be fortified to defend herself? I have come here to request your help with this problem. I beg you not to return Lady Cecily to her home until arrangements of some sort have been made. If we can find proof that Sir Eustace has done things he should be ashamed of, we can arm her with a powerful weapon."

"Enable her to blackmail him, you mean?" said Sherlock in the same soft and dangerous tone. "You should know I detest blackmail."

"But in a good cause—"

My plea was cut short, for that moment, quite to my astonishment, someone softly tapped at the back window just as I had done.

———————

A few moments later, Sherlock returned with his hand on the shoulder of the newcomer, a barefoot, grimy boy wearing the make-do motley of a street urchin, including a shapeless hat to hold down his shaggy hair.

". . . seen 'er, Mr. 'Olmes, right where you said she would be!" he was prattling. "And no mistake, pretty as that picture you showed us, even in a shawl an' togs too big for 'er. We all seen 'er, but then she hup and dispaired like a rabbit down a 'ole. We can't figure nohow—"

The boy's spate abated the moment he caught sight of me, and he stared at me in a most uncouth manner.

Not without reason, I reminded myself so as not to scowl at him.

Sherlock turned the boy by the shoulder to revert his attention to himself. "Where, exactly, did she disappear?"

"Why, by that 'ouse you pinted out to us, Mr. 'Olmes! She walked in beside it and never come out front nor back, neither. We was watching both ways."

"Very good, Wiggins. Well done." Releasing the lad, Sherlock rewarded him with some coinage. "Now run down to the corner and summon a cab." Sherlock saw the boy out of his flat by the conventional route, down the stairs and through the front door, to which he had a key. Then he returned to stride past me in the direction of his bedroom, saying, "I must get dressed."

"To go to Dr. Ragostin's residence?"

"To hasten to the abode of that fictitious personage, yes."

"I am coming with you."

"Nonsense, Enola." He shut the bedroom door behind him rather hard. Rather than shouting through it at him, I waited until he came out, in a remarkably brief time, impeccably clad, waistcoat and all.

"I am coming with you," I repeated.

"I work alone, Enola!"

"Alone, with Watson?"

"He is not such a pest as you."

"And I am not such a plodder as he. Are you afraid I might show some intelligence?"

My brother's eyebrows shot up, but, before he could respond, we both heard the front door open. I jumped up, rushed downstairs—meeting Wiggins on his way up—and got into the cab ahead of my brother, scattering coal dust every step of the way.

Right behind me, Sherlock ordered, "Out."

"In," I shot back. "I have the keys; how do you expect to enter the house without me? Would you care to admit to your frequent use of burglary?"

Stymied, he stood on the pavement beside, and, in the front of the hansom cab, I sat nearly as tall as he. Our eyes met. I tried to clear mine of anger, plea, any petty emotion.

"Do you wish to work with me or against me?" Sherlock asked, his voice quite neutral.

"That depends on your actions, my dear brother.

But mostly," I added, "I wish to see Cecily. We still haven't had a chance for a proper talk."

This disarmed him, I think, enabling him to roll his eyes at the folly of females. Although I could not see him clearly by the uncertain light of streetlamps and the cab's lanterns, I heard him sigh in a rather pronounced manner. Then, after giving the address to the cabbie, he climbed in to sit beside me. The horse started off, and we rattled away.

Although the cab jounced abominably, I laid my head back, closed my eyes, and pretended to rest, thinking it best to let Sherlock alone at that juncture. But pretense soon gave way to genuine slumber; I must have been wearier than I knew. I awoke to what seemed at first to be the sound of clamouring seagulls, and sat up, blinking and bewildered, to find the cab halted in front of our destination and mobbed by Sherlock's irregulars, their high-pitched voices gabbling all at once. "I saw 'er first!" "In the shadows she slunk like a right fox. Then—" "My mates and me, we 'id in the back." "Fat lot o' good yer did." "Then she dishappeared, like. She dint—"

Stepping out of the cab, Sherlock silenced the commotion with a benevolent gesture and a pocket purse. "You did admirably well. Here's your pay, lads. Dismissed." He handed out copper coins, and as each urchin received his, he ran off.

Meanwhile, I got myself out of the cab, out of the throng, and—no, I would not go around the corner of the house and show Sherlock the way into the secret door. He already knew quite enough. With my back turned to the street, I searched my bodice for the key to the front door and eventually found it just as Sherlock joined me.

"How inconvenient," he mused. "Why do women not use pockets?"

We did on occasion. But rather than honour his comment with a reply, I turned the key in the front door's lock, then opened the door and immediately turned up the gas for light, feeling a distinct danger that someone wakeful might hear us, come running with a blunderbuss, and shoot Sherlock and me before discovering we were not burglars.

"You constantly surprise me, Enola," said Sherlock

with a dry chuckle in his voice. "You wish to be *seen* in your besmirched pulchritude?"

No, I did not wish to be seen, not at all, but rather than admit it, I frowned at him, put a finger to my lips, and softly unlocked the door to the inner office. In there, I did not turn up the lights; I merely let in a shaft of illumination from the front room through the open door. Even before I saw Cecily, I knew she was there, as if we had a sister-sense between us.

With her shawl huddled around her, she nestled sound asleep on the davenport, looking like a waif, thin and pale.

Chapter the Fourteenth

Hours later, in the sunlit morning, she awoke to find me smiling down at her.

While she was still asleep, I had taken off my dreadful black dress and cleansed myself as best I could in the secret room, using up all the water I kept there in the process. I had brushed and brushed my hair, trying to get the coal dust out but succeeding only in spreading it rather more evenly. So I had braided my hair as best I could, arranged it on the top of my head, looked in the hand mirror, winced, then hid my hair altogether by wrapping Indian paisley-print cotton around it like a turban. With the ends hanging down over a fulsomely ruffled and flounced brick-red dress, it looked quite daring.

Meanwhile, Sherlock kept watch over Lady Cecily from an armchair. Rather than awakening the runaway lady to escort her home forthwith, he had let her sleep, a decision that credited him, in my mind, with at least some small degree of tenderheartedness. But he did not trust me enough to leave her with me.

When Cecily awoke, she did not at first see him, only me. With a glad cry, she sat up to hug me. "Enola!"

"I saw your mother just a few hours ago," I told her, hugging her back, "and she is in excellent health."

"Oh, thank you! I have been so worried." She nearly sobbed, and I knew at once that it was the right-handed persona of Cecily whom I held in my arms. "By bad luck, I encountered the girls with whom I used to go cycling, and they tried to get me to go home, and they told me Mama was sick with worry, not only about me, but also the little ones, my youngest brother and sister. It is torture to her to be separated from them. . . . Is Mama still locked in her rooms as helplessly as I—"

"In appearance, perhaps," sounded Sherlock's didactic voice. Cecily flinched and nearly screamed, startled and frightened because she had not known he was there. However, Sherlock went on smoothly. "Not in actuality. Your mother is not so helpless that she could not send a message to me, imploring me to find you."

"Phyllis took a message to my brother," I told Cecily, trying to calm her by patting her as if she were a scared horse. "Your mother and Phyllis have spare keys. Your father only *thinks* they are at his mercy."

"But can you not see they have no true freedom?" Pulling herself away from me, Cecily sat on the edge of the davenport facing Sherlock. "Please do not take me back there," she implored. "Please. Just take my mother a letter telling her I am all right—"

"But anyone can see you're not all right." Sherlock had steepled his hands. "When was the last time you ate? Have you run out of money?"

"Yes, but I'd rather starve on the streets than go back. If you knew my father— I beg you—"

"Tut, tut." Sherlock waved away her emotion with distaste, and to hush her, I think, he admitted, "I have not yet made up my mind what to do. Enola has brought some interesting considerations to my attention, Lady

Cecily, and I need to ask you some questions. But first, we had better order you something to eat."

"No, I am all aquiver; I cannot eat." Indeed, she visibly trembled with nerves. "Ask what you will."

"Very well. Lady Cecily, do you know anything about the funeral arrangements your father makes in the case of the unfortunate demise of a servant?"

She blinked, vacuous. "Pardon?"

"Wait," I told Sherlock. Crossing to the desk, I fetched pencils and a pad of foolscap paper. "Cecily, I would very much like you to please sketch my brother while he questions you." I drew a blind to let daylight play upon Sherlock's aquiline head. Looking at him, Cecily sat up straight, and her gaze grew intent. She took the darkest pencil in her left hand and made the first bold stroke, continuing to sketch in true, uncompromising lines, with no trace of a tremor in her hand or in her person.

"When the servants die, Cecily," I asked, "what happens?"

"Father seems to have some sort of special arrangement he shares with Aunt Otelia and Aunt Aquilla." Cecily kept drawing as she spoke.

Sherlock asked, "Sir Eustace disposes of the bodies for all three households?"

Disposes? Rather crudely put, I thought, but Cecily was now the forthright left-handed lady, unperturbed.

"Yes, and always has done since I can remember. During the diphtheria epidemic, he was very busy."

"And what does he do with the deceased servants?"

"I have no idea. How odd that I never had the curiosity to ask!"

Not so odd. They had kept her docile, right-handed, and nearly mute.

"But now that I come to think of it," she went on, "I have never attended a funeral for any servant. Father must have found a—a shortcut of some sort."

"Indeed." Then, for several moments, Sherlock studied Cecily intently. "Lady Cecily," he observed at last, "you seem to be left-handed."

She faltered to a halt, her drawing not quite finished. "I—I hadn't noticed."

"May I see?" Sherlock got up, came over to look at his portrait, then stared, amazed.

"And you thought I drew well," I teased him.

"Extraordinary! Acute, powerful, direct—one would think a man had done it."

"That is *not* a compliment," I said tartly.

He ignored me. "Lady Cecily, you are a true artist."

But the praise only added to her discomfiture. "I—am not—allowed . . ."

"Please, could you explain this to me?" He drew a paper from his waistcoat pocket and opened it. As he handed it to her, I saw it was the left-handed cipher of hers that I had given him. I inferred that he had eventually solved it and that—logical processes of deduction be praised—he had begun to understand what it meant for her to use her left hand.

Lady Cecily whispered, "I must have done that when I was . . . misbehaving."

"My dear lady, to be oneself is not misbehaviour, unless one is criminally inclined. Have you murdered anyone lately?"

She actually smiled, even laughed a little. "No."

"Then I suggest that Enola should order all of us some breakfast and that you should use your left hand to eat it."

He still has not decided what to do, I mused as I went

to ply the bell pull. Or, worse, he believed he must return Cecily to her unhappy family but could not bring himself to do it straightaway. Sherlock Holmes, by all Watson's accounts, was not likely to want breakfast or any other meal. I suspected that what he really wanted was time.

———

"We all love to slide down the laundry chute when Father is not home," Cecily said, brightening at the thought, after I reported my recent discoveries—about her father—and my perils to her. "Phyllis knew you would come out all right." Forking mushrooms and toast with her left hand clumsily but steadily, she devoured the excellent breakfast Mrs. Bailey had served us in the front office. "Do you think Mother will go along with your plan?"

"We did not have the opportunity to speak long, and it was Phyllis who gave me the names."

"You are being evasive, Enola," observed Sherlock gently enough. "Lady Theodora wanted nothing to do with it, did she?"

"She said neither yes nor no."

He sipped coffee judiciously. "It hardly matters, for with her or without her, your plan remains woefully incomplete."

"How so? Even if Lady Theodora cannot find sufficient spine to confront her husband, Cecily can still tell her father that she knows he has sold bodies to the dissecting rooms, not to mention the dentists, and that she will make this fact public unless he betters his behaviour."

Sherlock shook his head in his usual superior way. "He will ask her what proof she has, but she has none. And even if she did, he need only lock her in her room again, guarding against invasion by bow and arrow, to render her helpless. No, you need a third party in the transaction, and you need documentation, a compromising paper of some sort."

"Would you care to act as that third party and acquire such documentation?"

"I will not, must not, cannot dirty my hands with blackmail."

"It's not really blackmail," I said.

"Excuse me." Cecily leaned close to me to murmur in my ear, "Nature calls. Is it possible—"

"Of course." I rang, and Joddy, for once in his life, appeared promptly. "Show our guest to the kitchen," I directed him, "and have Mrs. Bailey help her." The water closet had been installed at the very back of the house, of course, as nearly as possible out-of-doors, because of the smell.

As Cecily walked away, I noticed how straight she stood and how surely she walked when she was her truer self, the left-handed lady. I had to hide a smile, for I rather suspected what she was about to do.

After she exited, I resumed debating with Sherlock. "It's not really blackmail. Money as such will not be sought."

"Only financial support during separation? Or perhaps the expense of an alienist for Lady Cecily?" Obstinately, Sherlock shook his head. "As soon as she reappears from the nether regions, I am leaving and taking her with me." He raised a hand to halt my protests. "I promise you I will insist on seeing Lady Theodora, and if at all possible, Sir Eustace, to impress upon him that the eyes of society are watching him."

"He will lock Cecily in her bedroom the moment you leave."

"Perhaps. I hope not. But if you are so set on your plan, Enola, pursue it yourself. If you can bring it off, you will be just as effective a few weeks or months from now. Certainly, Lady Cecily can survive her father that long."

"Find proof and documentation, you mean."

"Yes."

"Hypothetically speaking, how should I proceed?"

So questioned, he could not resist expounding upon possible sources of information and courses of action. Thus I held him in conversation for quite a length of time before he suddenly demanded, "Enola, why is Lady Cecily taking so long?"

Chapter the Fifteenth

Several hours later, back in my room at the Professional Women's Club, having taken a thoroughgoing bath and washed the coal dust out of my hair with the help of a maid, I put on a dressing gown; swaddled my disorderly, wet head in a dry towel; and went to bed. It is quite a bad idea to go to sleep with wet hair, for it dries into the most extraordinary kinks and serpentines; one can go about for days looking like Medusa. But that could not be helped; I desperately needed sleep. I was drained, spent, exhausted from having been up all night and also from the rigours of dealing with Sherlock after he discovered Lady Cecily was gone.

To give him all due credit, his anger manifested mainly in the hue of his nose, which went bone white. He did not curse, and he did not shout or even raise his voice, but he was plainly furious—mostly at himself, I think, for having expected tame obedience from Cecily. "I had not imagined there could be another one as ungovernable as you, Enola," he snapped before exiting in a most uncertain frame of mind.

But Mrs. Bailey and Mrs. Fitzsimmons were even more so. Angry, that is. Shortly after Sherlock slammed the front door, they had come to me quite strident because they had found their purses, which they kept on chairs in the kitchen, emptied of pounds, shillings, and pence. In each purse had been left an IOU for the exact amount taken, with my name on it. These clumsily written missives had been left not by me, of course, but by Cecily, who knew I never lacked funds and would not mind paying. Indeed, as I reimbursed Fitzsimmons and Bailey, thereby calming them, I rejoiced for two reasons: Cecily had obtained sufficient money to stay on the run for a few more days, and she was still using her left hand even though it made writing difficult for her.

I returned to my lodgings in the Professional Women's Club with a serene demeanor concealing my concerns for Lady Cecily. So long as she remained confident and left-handed, I did not fear for her. But as she had been quite overwhelmingly brought up docile and right-handed, she might at any time revert to being meek and helpless. Even as I closed my eyes for a well-deserved nap, this thought troubled me, and so did the thought of my brother. Deep in my heart, I felt an unaccustomed ache on account of him. Because I felt guilty? No; examining my conduct, I found that I could not have acted differently. But he was angry. I ached because he was angry. I was so new, you see, to having brothers, having a family, that I felt afraid of—of losing him. We had not quarreled, not really, but still I felt miserable.

It was, however, a familiar misery: that of being alone. Indeed, my name, backwards, spells "alone." Many a time I had gone to sleep feeling lonely, so, without difficulty, I did so once again.

I slept so soundly and so long that I missed dinner but awoke, ravenous, sometime after everyone else had gone to bed. Carrying a lamp rather like Diogenes searching for an honest man, I padded downstairs in my dressing gown and slippers to the empty and silent kitchen, where I set my light on the table, turned around to look for something to eat, and nearly screamed at my own shadow. During my sleep, I had shed the towel that had wrapped my head, and now I looked a fright in the most literal sense of the word; locks of my hair writhed, serpentine, in all directions, and then they actually seemed to move! I covered my mouth with my hands, choking back a small shriek, before I realized the effect was caused by a light moving behind me.

"What utterly stunning hair!" said Lady Vienna; I knew her voice even before I turned to see her come in, looking paradoxically girlish in a butterfly kimono with her hair trailing in two silver braids. Setting her candle on the table beside my lantern, she continued, "Really, my dear, it is most artistic!" Her limpid eyes glowed with what seemed to be genuine admiration.

"You look like one of those unruly flowers, what*ever* are they called, so attractive to bees. . . ." She clasped her hands and marveled at me with her gaze as if I were on display in the Louvre.

Hardly knowing what to say, I blurted, "I'm so sorry, Lady Vienna; did I awaken you?"

"Oh no, dear, no! Not at all. I hardly sleep at all anymore, and I often come here to mess about in the middle of the night. The cooks forgive my depredations." Quite at home, she turned up the gas and blew out her candle. "I was about to make myself some coddled eggs. Are you hungry?"

"Starving. I missed both luncheon and dinner."

"Merciful heavens, you live a most unregulated life!" Opening one of the ovens, she pulled out of its black belly a basket covered with a white linen napkin. This she handed to me, commenting, "The cooks have kindly let me know where they hide the goodies."

Goodies, indeed! Jam-stuffed pastries, buns, sweet biscuits, muffins, iced cakes, and cookies seemingly without end greeted my eyes, inviting me to partake. And, seating myself at the kitchen table, partake I did, in plenty and at blissful length, entirely forgetting my manners until Lady Vienna placed a napkin, a fork, and a plateful of hot coddled eggs in front of me.

"Oh!" I wailed. "I am a hopeless case! I despair of myself! I should have been helping you."

"Nonsense," she said with greatest good cheer, sitting at the table with me to eat her own eggs. "If I'd needed your help, I would have asked for it."

Those words echoed within the apparent emptiness of my mind as we ate. If I needed help . . .

"Thank you for the eggs," I said sincerely as I was wiping my mouth afterwards. Coddled eggs were a treat, for it is an exercise in patience to cook them, constantly stirring them in simmering milk until the mixture attains the texture of cottage cheese. "I have never tasted better."

"You are quite welcome, my mysterious young lady," she replied, smiling with unusual warmth. "What mischief are you contemplating now?"

She must have seen my thoughts on my face! And I could not help responding in kind to her smile. "It is most salubrious, our meeting here like this," I admitted, "for I want to speak with you quite privately about a matter of some moment."

"Certainly, my dear." Placing her empty plate aside,

she faced me, eyes sparkling with fun, and saved me a great deal of footling about by asking, "How is Lady Cecily getting along?"

"Because of the way her personality changes from moment to moment, there is no telling!" All earnest concern, I hurtled on. "She would be better off at home, if only Sir Eustace could be managed. I have received affirmation of those rumours you confided to me; Cecily says her father disposes of his sisters' deceased servants in the same dubious way he does his own, and Lady Theodora's maid gave me the names of three of the latter. If we had not been interrupted, I am sure she would have given me more."

"I have heard you came home with coal dust in your hair," Lady Vienna remarked.

"How word does get about. But yes, quite so. I am not at all welcome in the Alastair residence." I paused while she drew her smiling conclusions. "But I must go there again, for, as you once told me yourself, Lady Vienna, I need proof. I must lay my hands on compromising documents of some sort. If Sir Eustace keeps records of his transactions with the dissecting rooms, I hope to purloin them. And I must ask: Would you be willing to help me?"

She raised her eyebrows. "How, exactly?"

I outlined a plan that I think she found a bit daring, for she only pondered me without answering when I asked again whether she would help.

"Sir Eustace himself has never seen me," I added. "The butler has, but I am capable of disguising myself quite convincingly, and you could see to it that all their attention remained upon yourself."

Again she studied me in silence.

"Lady Vienna, surely you can see that we would be morally in the right, although—"

She held up a hand to silence me. "I don't mind breaking the law. I have done so many times in the interest of women's rights. What gives me pause is, I have never met a creature such as you. A Perditorian? So young? And the risks you take . . . Why?"

I knew exactly how to make her understand. Since the day I had first encountered her, I had wanted to tell her something, and this was the perfect opportunity. Warmth swelled my heart and rose to my face; I felt myself smiling widely. "Because I am my mother's daughter," I said. "My full name is Enola Holmes, and my mother was Eudoria Vernet Holmes."

Having known Mum well, Lady Vienna required no further explanation of me. "Oh!" she gasped, hands to her mouth, and then she cried in a different way, "OH!" and lifted her arms like wings to fly to me. "Oh, when we were young, she was my best friend!"

I welcomed her embrace, hugged her in return, and we both started crying.

———————

After we had finished having a sniffle and a very good talk, I went back to bed feeling like a drowsy child who has been well fed, kissed, cuddled, and tucked in. Even though Mum had seldom done any of those things, I felt as if I had her back, in a roundabout way, for Lady Vienna Steadwell was a kindred spirit with Lady Eudoria Vernet Holmes. While it had been hard to tell her that Mum was no longer with us, she had felt, as I did, how marvelous it was that Mum had spent the last year of her life happy and free with the Gypsies, wandering the countryside unconstrained by corsets or society. And like me, she found it fitting and poetic that Mum had been laid to rest in a Gypsy burial to go ride the starry dark horses, her gravesite secret and unmarked.

"Dear Eudoria," she said, "was a true original, an individual, a woman quite beyond compare."

But what she said next touched me even more.

"Yet, my dear Enola, I am sure she made a very difficult mother."

"Wonderful and impossible." I could not say more. I had thought I was finished crying, but I wept anew.

Wonderful and impossible. Rather like Sherlock, I thought as I lay drowsy from a surfeit of sweet pastries and emotions. I felt a pang of distress because Sherlock was perhaps angry with me, and decided that I needed to see him as soon as possible, perhaps even tomorrow, as soon as Lady Vienna and I had finished "calling" upon the Alistairs.

Chapter the Sixteenth

My preparations began the next day directly after luncheon. I chose my newest, most fashionable afternoon calling costume of violet faille with long, slim sleeves puffed at the shoulder and a very modern skirt swept back from a centre panel of lilac, that colour being also repeated in scalloped trim on my bodice. I had to summon a maid to help me with my hair, which no amount of brushing could seem to quell. She exclaimed over it, ran a wet comb through it, and managed to pin it into a coif of sorts that I could cover with my hat. Luckily, the latest hats served that purpose admirably, being of heroic proportions. Mine looked rather like a purple channel marker with aigrettes, poufs of voile, and a swooping brim.

Dismissing the maid, I then applied some subtle colour to my lips, cheekbones, and eyes. Wearing my new jacket and my best kid gloves, and carrying my fanciest parasol, I promenaded downstairs to meet Lady Vienna.

Even though I had never seen her in formal attire, I was not at all surprised to find that she had outdone me.

"Is that a *Worth* gown?" I exclaimed of her costume, which was a wonder to behold, a holly-green taffeta bodice over a cream brocade skirt striped with embroidered sprays of roses, gathered with green bows in front but trailing cream silk pleated "sweepers" behind.

"When I promise full fig, I deliver full fig." With one daintily gloved hand, she raised a lorgnette to her eyes as if she could not see me otherwise, while, with the other hand, she serenely plied quite an ornate but peculiar fan. "Heavens, what a decadent hat, and how ever did you manage such a facial transformation! My dear Aubergina, I would not know you!" We had agreed that, for the day, I should be her "niece" Aubergina

Parthe Steadwell. (She had no such niece; indeed, we based "Aubergina" on the French word for "eggplant.") After surveying me, she nodded approval, the ribbons and plumes on her own outrageous hat bobbing. "I do believe we are ready."

A hired carriage awaited us, not a cab, and it was a carriage the queen herself would not have been ashamed to ride in, complete with a coachman in a cocked hat and a footman wearing his absurdly traditional uniform, including white wig, knee breeches, white stockings, and buckle shoes. Odd, how the fancy-dress clothing of one century becomes the servant's garb of the next. What would an alienist make of that?

Many faces watched from the windows of the Professional Women's Club as the footman attended us with great ceremony, handing us up to sit enclosed within our mobile throne, and as a matched pair of bay horses trundled us away. But once we were out of sight of our audience, I tapped the roof of our carriage with my parasol, signaling a halt.

Because of the roiling London traffic, this manoeuvre took the coachman some time to perform, even though his carriage gave him precedence over broughams,

Victorias, landaus, and other vehicles of lesser rank. Once we had stopped rolling, I heard the footman jump down and trot around to open the door and look up at Lady Vienna and me, quite blank with surprise.

"Have the driver secure the reins and come here, also," I told him.

Once this was done, I spoke to two blank faces instead of one. "We wish to pay in advance," I told them, "and alert you that we may possibly have some need for your assistance or cooperation, not knowing quite what may happen this afternoon."

"Despite appearances, this is not to be one's usual social call," put in Lady Vienna serenely. "May we depend upon you gentlemen?" she asked as I handed them their fee and she reached across to add a handsome gratuity for each of them. No longer blank, both of them nodded so eagerly that powder flew from their wigs. Evidently, Lady Vienna and I had lent novelty to their day.

"Drive on," I said, smiling, for I, too, felt the zesty allure of mischief.

We did not stop again until, on the tranquil street

of a residential neighbourhood, we pulled up in front of the Alistairs' stately Georgian brick home.

The footman handed us down, accompanied us to the door, and plied the lion's-head knocker for us, all with the most excellent servility. Lady Vienna, as we had agreed, had taken the lead, calling card in her gloved hand. When the stone-faced butler opened the door, I stood back, my chin tucked to obscure my face beneath my hat brim, and simpered.

Without wasting any time upon civility, the butler announced, "Lady Theodora is seeing no one," and began to shut the door in our faces.

"Indeed, Smythe?" chided Lady Vienna, her crisp invocation of his name instantly turning him to a metaphorical pillar of salt. "You were not taught to be so abrupt when you were in training at Earl Blackwater's. Kindly tell Sir Eustace that Lady Steadwell and her niece, the Honourable Aubergina Steadwell, wish to see him."

All then followed in due course. The unfortunate Smythe took her card upon his salver, its silver surface visibly shaking in his hands, and showed us into the parlour after we had dismissed our footman. He seated us in two huge plush armchairs flanking an elaborately carved Carrera marble fireplace, took my parasol to set it in the elephant-foot stand, then vanished. Lady Vienna sat quite at her ease in her overstuffed chair, languidly fanning herself for no reason, smiling at me.

I whispered, "That is a fan worthy of the Arabian Nights. What on earth is it made of?"

"Aside from the carved ivory sticks? Point lace, garnets, and crocodile skin."

Luckily, no response was required from me, for a roaring voice sounded from some other room in the house: "Smythe, I ordered you not to let anyone in!"

"Darling Eustace." Lady Vienna's smile subtly changed to become a bit crocodilian, like her fan.

A few moments later, Sir Eustace entered the parlour, and perhaps he thought he was scowling, but, to me, he appeared to pout.

"Ah, you are surprised to see me, my dear boy!" Graciously, Lady Vienna extended her gloved hand to be kissed. "You know I have always been nothing if not outspoken, so let me explain myself at once: I am making the rounds of all my lifelong acquaintance for a purpose. You see, being of an age soon to slough off this mortal body, I must decide as to the disposition of my worldly goods."

Sir Eustace, who had been glaring down at her extended hand, quite suddenly changed demeanor, bowed, and pressed it to his lips.

"May I present my niece, or more precisely, the daughter of a deceased niece: the Honourable Aubergina Treadwell, who has become my companion during my declining years."

Although I did not think Sir Eustace could possibly recognize me, having never actually seen me—still, my heart pounded as I extended my hand, murmuring something inaudible and tilting my face downwards in feigned maidenly confusion. But the cold peck he bestowed upon my glove nearly made me smile, so plainly did it demonstrate that he considered me his competition for Lady Vienna's fortune. Turning his back on me, he seated himself facing us, one elbow on the parlour's inevitable pedestal table, affecting a manly attitude.

Little did he know that, as Lady Vienna had merrily told me, she intended to disburse her fortune whilst she still lived until she was rich only in memories.

At once, she began to deploy these, recalling to Sir Eustace episodes of his childhood she had observed when she had been the debutante daughter of family friends. With each of her recollections, including the arrow-in-derriere one, he looked less poised and more dyspeptic. Judging by the gleam in her celadon-green eyes, she enjoyed discomfiting him, but she moved on in accordance with the programme she and I had planned, asking how his sisters were, then commiserating with him about the illness of "your lovely wife, Lady Theodora. How unfortunate that we shall not be able to meet her."

Actually, I had warned Lady Vienna that Lady Theodora might recognize my face.

"Under normal circumstances, Eustace, I suppose your wife is quite a capable manager? She must be, as you have such a brood of children, but may I see for myself?" As if it were the most natural thing in the world that she should wish to examine the household accounts, Lady Vienna arose and swept out of the parlour, across the hallway, and into the library while I followed like a baby duck. So majestically did she progress that the omnipresent butler leapt to bring her a chair, and Sir Eustace scurried to unlock for her the secretary, an item of furniture as inevitable as pedestal tables in upper-class households. Grander than a roll-top desk, the cherrywood secretary loomed, glassed-in shelves above, locked drawers below, and, in between, pigeon-holes and secret compartments secured behind a well-polished fold-up writing surface.

Sir Eustace unlocked this first, then the drawers. Seated at the desk prepared for her use, Lady Vienna plucked the current ledger from the drawer, raised her lorgnette to her eyes, glanced through several pages of numbers in columns, then took the ledger from the previous year, 1888, and scanned it, her eyebrows arching higher by the moment. "You certainly are sailing close to the wind," she remarked, staring severely at Sir Eustace. "Being a modern woman, I cannot approve of such an outdated personage as an aristocrat living beyond his means. Otherwise, I would not trouble myself to look beyond my own relations in order to bequeath my fortune. My intention is to leave it to someone who exhibits a brisk spirit of capitalist enterprise—"

"I have made quite enterprising sales and investments," interrupted Sir Eustace, his plump body quivering like that of a bird dog on point, his small features somewhat enlarged and improved by distress of mind.

Lady Vienna peered at him over her lorgnette. "Sales and investments regarding what?"

"Regarding, er, art." Sir Eustace slid open one of the secretary's "secret" panels and removed from it a pocket journal covered in red leather. Rather hesitantly, he handed it to Lady Vienna, who opened it to the first page.

"Timothy Burke," she read aloud, maintaining the most admirable composure while I barely kept myself from gasping. "I have never heard of him. Is he an artist?"

"No, he was the subject. I deal in, ah, portraiture."

"Well, he fetched quite a tidy sum. This notation, BSC, signifies a collection?"

As she talked, I moved forwards ever so casually to stand by her shoulder. Because I had kept silence, the merest satellite in Lady Vienna's solar system, no one, not the maid or the butler or Sir Eustace, either, seemed to notice.

"Um, er, yes," Sir Eustace was saying.

"Imogen Saunders was a female subject?" She handed the pocket ledger to me while still engaging Sir Eustace in conversation. "And her portrait went to the same collection?"

"Yes, um . . ." Before Sir Eustace realized what was happening, I was halfway across the library. "Wait! Stop!" he squealed, so I ran. I regretted being obliged to abandon my best parasol, but one must have one's priorities. Thanks to modern dresses that no longer swept the floor, I could run, even sprint, without needing to pick up my skirt. Therefore, when Smythe, the butler, jumped in front of me to bar the door, I was able, without slackening my pace, to whip my dagger out of my bodice and raise it—not truly menacing; I had no intention of taking his life. If he had not moved out of my way (which he did, with an undignified exclamation and great alacrity), I might perhaps have cut him superficially, nothing more.

I burst into the hallway, and, as I turned towards the front door, I caught a sidelong glimpse of Lady Vienna following close behind me but turning the other way, providing a diversion.

Baronet and butler yelled in counterpoint, "Help!" "Thief!" "Catch her!" "Stop her!" "Stop—Lady Vienna?"

"I am going upstairs to visit with your wife, Sir Eustace," she sang. Indeed, she sounded as if she were already on the stairs as I plunged out the front door and pelted towards the carriage, precious red-covered evidence in hand.

Although they had been warned that something like this might happen, the coachman and the footman sat ogling. So, rather than trying to climb into the coach, I flung myself onto the driver's seat along with them and ordered, "Go!"

Gathering his reins, the coachman stammered, "B-b-but the other lady—"

"She will be fine!" We had agreed beforehand that she would fend for herself at this point, and I would have wagered on Lady Vienna against any number of baronets. Grabbing the whip from its socket, I cracked it over the horses' backs, making them leap forwards. "Go, and keep going, and be smart about it!"

Heavens, I sounded nearly as commanding as Sherlock. We went.

Chapter the Seventeenth

Answering the door at 221 Baker Street, Mrs. Hudson beamed upon seeing me. "My, don't you look nice, Miss Enola! But I'm sorry to say Mr. Holmes has gone out."

Gone out! When I had jumped off of the carriage in the middle of a crowded street so that I could not be traced, dodged dray-horses and carriage-horses in order to catch a tram to St. Pancras Station, then braved the underground in my stylish clothing, then hired a cab to hasten to Sherlock, he dared to be *out*? When I stood on his doorstep with Sir Eustace's little red ledger of ill-gotten gains hidden in my bust amplifier, where I seemed to feel it burning my bosom? How dared Sherlock be out?

"When do you expect him back?"

"He didn't say, but he wore his city suit, so perhaps he was going to an afternoon recital?" Mrs. Hudson contemplated me with her usual patient anxiety. "Would you care to come in and wait, Miss Enola?"

"No, thank you, Mrs. Hudson. My business is pressing. . . . Mrs. Hudson, would you happen to know where Mr. Holmes takes valuable evidence for photographic duplication?"

Blinking, she admitted she did not, and I went away fuming. But once I remembered *Enola, think,* I hired another cab and went to call on Dr. Watson, whom I could indubitably find, as his office hours were in the afternoon. In all my purple glory I sailed past the humbler souls seated in his waiting room and rapped on his inner door. Blinking, much like Mrs. Hudson, he opened it. From behind him, his patient, a palsied old woman, glared at me.

"I'm dreadfully sorry to interrupt," I said insincerely before putting to him the same question I had asked Mrs. Hudson.

He knew the answer, but as he wrote down an address for me on a page out of his prescription book, he said, "Frankly, my dear Enola, they are not likely to take you seriously. It would be far better if Holmes—"

"He is out gallivanting," I interrupted with some heat.

Watson's eyes took on a contemplative sheen. "Yes. Yes, of course, he would be at the Strand this afternoon."

Such and such a violinist was playing such and such a sonata; I did not listen, hurrying back to my cab, offering the driver a sovereign if he conveyed me to the Strand before the programme let out.

He got me there just as the doors were opening. And, in the crowd that issued forth, I mingled quite inconspicuously, for all the ladies were "in full fig" quite as much as I was.

Due to his stork-like qualities, especially when wearing his top hat, it was not hard to locate Sherlock. However, it was rather more difficult to get him to notice me. Fluttering a handkerchief at him only made him look away and lengthen his stride to escape what appeared to be an attractive female on the hunt. Only by deserting my dignity and trotting after him did I catch him—with my gloved hand on his arm. "Sherlock!"

With greatest reluctance, he turned to face me, removing his hat, before he realized who I was. Then his reaction was mixed. Alas, there are few words in the English language to encompass simultaneous but opposite emotions; indeed, I can think of only one: bittersweet. Could my brother's facial expression, in which vexation mingled with fraternal affection, perhaps be called grumpyglad?

"What on earth is it now, Enola?"

His greeting was hardly cordial, but, quite spontaneously, I smiled. "It is not my fault, Sherlock, that you expected Cecily to report meekly back to you like an obedient young lady."

"I suppose not," he admitted ungraciously. "But what brings you here, Enola, dressed to distraction beneath a preposterous hat?"

"No more preposterous than your stovepipe," I said as he put his tall silk topper back onto his head. But then, more softly, I told him, "I need you to escort me to this mysterious friend of yours who has a darkroom in his cellar, Sherlock. After which we must go find Cecily."

Sherlock sent a boy to get us a growler—that is to say, a four-wheeled, enclosed cab—and when it rolled up to us, to my surprise, I recognized the horse—Brownie—and the driver. Usually, he drove a hansom.

I blurted, "Harold!"

"Miss Enola?" He sounded as surprised as I, never having seen me in such violet splendor. Or in such top-hatted company. He snatched off his bowler and bowed his head to Sherlock.

"My brother," I explained, quite irregularly, as one does not customarily introduce one's family to one's cabdriver.

Sherlock helped me into the cab. "I am not even going to ask," he commented in the tone of one who has just rolled his eyes. "Harold, is it?" But he gave Harold the address courteously enough.

The cab moved off, and, in its carriage-like privacy, I showed Sherlock my prize: Sir Eustace's pocket journal. Having not yet had a good look at it myself, I sat beside him to study it. By its evidence, Sir Eustace had sold thirty-seven "portraits."

"How in heaven's name did you come into possession of this?" Sherlock demanded.

"Feminine wiles," I told him. "What does 'BSC' mean?"

"'Battersea Surgical Conservatory.' Sir Eustace appears to have excellent connexions."

Our stop at the photographer's establishment took very little time, as Sherlock was accustomed to dealing with him and he could be trusted. We left the pocket journal for him to duplicate, arranged to call back for it in a few hours, then returned to our waiting cab. "Harold," I told my friend, "we need you to take us to the East End by way of Aldgate Pump."

The gentle reader must understand that the East End is London's worst slum, the stalking ground of Jack the Ripper. Few cabbies ventured there. But ours, providentially, was Harold.

"Anything you say, Miss Enola."

Sherlock looked quizzical as we resumed our seats, but I chose not to explain.

"So, my dear brother," I said as we settled in for a torturous drive through late-day London traffic, "how goes it with the case of the European royalty, the destitute divorcée, and the pink circus poodle?"

He waved the question away. "Long since solved.

Would that it were as easy to penetrate your mind and its machinations."

"Heavens, I am not so difficult to keep up with." Briefly, I told him what I had done since we last met, ignoring his occasional exclamations of outrage or despair. But when we reached the Aldgate Pump, all eighteen feet tall of it, surely London's most monstrous monument to progress and hygiene, with water pouring out of the mouth of a brass wolf's head—when we came to this landmark at the boundary of the City and the Great Unwashed, I cut my account short, stuck my head out the window, and called to Harold, "Proceed slowly, please." Then I instructed Sherlock, "You watch for her from your side, and I'll do the same from mine."

"Is that *it*?" he said in heightened tones. "Is this the entirety of your plan to find Lady Cecily?"

"No, of course not. But were she to be walking, it would be a shame if we missed her, would it not?"

With an exhalation that sounded very much like a snort, Sherlock applied himself to his window.

Here the street traffic was very different than it was in the City. While we met few horse-drawn vehicles, the cobblestones teemed with pedestrians and vendors of every description—ginger beer sellers, dealers in meat pies, kippered herring, apples, muffins, hot sweet buns, et cetera, plus a poultry huckster with live birds dangling by their trussed feet from a yoke that extended across his shoulders. I must admit I rather stared at him and at buxom girls swinging from streetlamps by ropes, which some manner of monkey must have strung up. But, mostly, I watched for Cecily in a brown suit and, most likely, an inexpensive boater hat.

Although I saw many young women answering this description, I did not see her. Nor did Sherlock.

However, when I caught sight of a certain building, I thumped on the ceiling for Harold to stop. "Wait for us, please," I told him after I got out, as Sherlock joined me on the pavement.

"Yer can count on me, Miss Enola. An', um, sir. Mr. 'Olmes."

While all the street denizens stared at Sherlock and me (for, in city suit and "full fig," we stood out like orchids in a daisy patch), we stared at the building, a large but plain brick edifice, made remarkable only by poles that towered above the roof with heavy black wires attached to them. The wrought-iron lettering over the door proclaimed: EAST LONDON TELEPHONE EXCHANGE.

I took Sherlock's arm. "In we go."

"On what pretext?"

"We look like aristocrats; we need none except curiosity. They will hope we are potential subscribers. Do you have a monocle to peer through?"

The corners of his mouth twitched as if he might actually smile, but then he assumed the bored air of a lordly personage. I clung to his arm with one hand and hoisted my skirt daintily with the other as we ascended the steps. Then he bowed me through double oak doors, and I stepped into a peculiar place that felt rather like the hybrid offspring of a factory and a barn. Partitions divided it into three wide aisles, along the sides of which sat women on tall chairs facing the walls like so many cows at their stanchions, each wearing a white apron over her street clothes. Instead of the din of machinery, I heard polite voices and sounds rather like the stridulations of summertime insects. Something would buzz, and then a woman would reach to pluck a conical device from a peg and apply its open end to her ear.

A man in spats, obviously a manager, approached us and bowed. "May I help you?"

What Sherlock told him I do not know, for, quite intently, I continued to watch the women. Holding the conical device to one ear, they spoke, each into her own circular hole in the partition. Then, with their other hand, they wrote something down, laid the pencil aside, and reached up to manipulate a bewilderment of devices situated upon the wall in front of them.

All but one of them used her right hand to do this.

I felt a warm grip squeeze my heart. I walked towards the left-handed girl.

Wisely, Sherlock remained behind.

Yes, it was Cecily; no one could mistake that perfect profile. Crouching beside her hard wooden chair, I smiled up at her.

At first, intent on her work, she did not notice me. "I'm sorry, but the subscriber is not picking up," she said into her stanchion. "Would you care to try again later? Very well. Good evening." But, after she took the hearing device away from her ear and hung it on its peg, she looked at me, and her face lit up. "Enola!"

"I have good news for you," I said, not calling her by

name, for I did not expect she was using her real name here. "At least I hope it is good news. Can you come with me?"

"But my shift will not be over until eight o'clock. I will lose my job."

"How long each day must you work?"

"Twelve hours." Then she repeated in a different tone, "Twelve hours! And the match girls work fourteen! I never knew a day could be so long."

"Come with me?" I asked again, and this time she stood up with a decided lift of her chin, took her apron off, and threw it at her chair. Walking with me towards the door, she hesitated when she saw Sherlock. But he nodded at her in such a reassuring way, so brimming with the milk of human kindness, that I could scarcely believe it.

Cecily nodded back, and just as the streetlamps were being lit, the three of us exited the East London Telephone Exchange. Some gawkers in the crowded street jeered—we ignored them—and Harold's honest, homely face showed distinct signs of relief when he saw us.

Chapter the Eighteenth

"Wait." Cecily halted short of the cab, addressing Sherlock. "Mr. Holmes, do you intend to deliver me back into the hands of my father?"

"No," he said with a wry look, "I intend to violate the laws of nature by delivering your father into the hands of you and your mother."

"Are you serious?"

"Yes, and Enola is even more so." Bowing, he offered his hand, and she accepted his assistance into the cab.

"What does he mean?" she demanded as I climbed in to sit beside her.

So, as the cab carried us back to the photographer's establishment, I explained. As each stage of the explanation seemed to demand another, this took some time. Lady Cecily listened intently but remained thoughtful, not embracing my proposal as enthusiastically as I had hoped.

"Has Papa truly committed a crime?" she appealed, which surprised me, because I had not thought she could retain any affection for her father. But having had no father since I was four years old, perhaps I failed to appreciate the parental bond.

"He has mostly committed an embarrassment," I replied. "He should have sent his deceased servants to their families for burial. Instead, he sold their bodies to dissecting rooms and—and others. It would be a dreadful scandal if it came out."

"Sir Eustace has perhaps stepped on the skirts of the law," put in Sherlock, who had remained remarkably silent heretofore. "But, quite naturally, the servants' families have not pressed charges. They know their place. You need not fear your father will stand in the dock. So, Lady Cecily, do you accept this metaphorical sword to hold over his head?"

"Yes," she said, "gladly," although she remained grave and quiet rather than rejoicing.

"Then I suggest you decide what your conditions will be."

"Conditions?"

"Not conditions of surrender," I explained, annoyed. "Rather, stipulations of victory. Rules regarding your father's future behaviour. Demands."

"Demands?" Her voice sounded faint. I tried to study her face, but there was not enough light within the cab, as it was growing dark outside.

"Cecily," I said with some asperity, "come back, please."

"I, um, I'm sorry, but I don't understand." She sounded as meek as a mouse. Evidently, sometime during the cab ride, she had ceased being left-handed.

I made the list of demands for her, waiting with her in the cab whilst Sherlock went into the photographer's establishment for the prints of the pages of the red-bound pocket journal, not to speak of the original. Of course, I carried paper and pencil in my bust amplifier as usual, and I wrote by the light of a streetlamp:

1) Neither Lady Theodora, Lady Cecily, nor any of the latter's sisters are ever again to be confined to bedrooms or boudoirs or deprived of any necessities such as clothing, food, and drink.

2) Sir Eustace is at all times to treat his wife with respect and to consult her regarding any discipline of the children.

3) Should Lady Cecily make arrangements to live elsewhere than at her family residence, Sir Eustace is not to stand in the way of those arrangements.

4) Should Lady Cecily wish to consult an alienist

I had got this far when Sherlock returned with a small red journal and a large sheaf of photographs. "My friend promises to retain the plates for us in case these ever come to harm," he said, handing me the pocket journal and brandishing the photographs, "but have you considered where we ought to keep them?"

"I had thought I could hide them in Dr. Ragostin's office. But there is a difficulty." With a tilt of my head, I directed his attention to Cecily, who remained politely oblivious of our conversation, as if it were our business and did not concern her. "She has lapsed into being right-handed again. And in that condition she would lead her father straight to them."

Sitting opposite Lady Cecily in the cab, Sherlock studied her for several minutes, and I fancied he might wish he had a pipe full of shag tobacco to suck upon, for she was a problem.

Eventually, he said, "I apologize that I did not at first believe you, Enola."

"How could you believe anything so extraordinary? But now you see the flaw in my plan: Unless Cecily can be cured, she cannot be counted upon to stand up for herself. Someone is going to have to speak and act on her behalf. Not just tonight, but for a long time to come."

"Lady Theodora has been her daughter's advocate," said Sherlock without much conviction.

"Yes, and she has been defeated. It was her maid who gave me the names. Lady Theodora herself acted quite horrified."

"Well, if not Lady Theodora, then who?"

"You."

Without hesitation and without raising his voice, he replied, "I cannot, Enola. I cannot and will not take part in a blackmail scheme."

"But if one does not demand money—"

"It is still extortion. And one is, indirectly, demanding money." He nodded at my list, which he had been reading upside down. "The expense of support, should Lady Theodora choose a separation, or the cost of an alienist—"

I began to fume, and my voice rose, throwing sparks. "Call it what you will—blackmail, extortion—can you think of any bullying man who deserves it more than Sir Eustace? Can you not make an exception for a good cause?"

"No." Oddly, he sounded quite gentle, as if he regretted disappointing me. "No, Enola, not even for you."

I opened my mouth, but I found nothing fiery to say, so I shut it again.

"You must take care of your own business," Sherlock added more coolly.

Enola, you will do quite well on your own. Mum's voice in my mind.

I sighed, then considered how best to proceed.

"Yes, you're correct, of course, Sherlock." To my own surprise, I sounded assured and reasonable. Putting my head out the window again, I directed the long-suffering Harold to drive to my place of lodging, where I would conceal the shocking evidence for the time being.

In my room at the Professional Women's Club, I hid Sir Eustace's pocket journal and the photographic copies of its pages beneath my mattress—hardly the most ingenious arrangement but safe from the predations of any males, or any females, either, until the next time the bed was made. I must make sure to move journal and photographs to a more cleverly secret location before then.

Straightening up after rearranging the bedcover, I caught sight of myself in the mirror and frowned at my lavender-bedecked reflection. My hat was indeed a ludicrous affair. How could anyone, far less Sir Eustace, take such a popinjay of fashion seriously?

There was no time to change my dress, for the cab and Sherlock and Cecily were waiting for me. But I wrenched off the hat by main force, sending hatpins and hairpins flying, and then I bent over in order to let gravity assist me as I plucked out more hairpins and combed out the rest with my fingers. When I stood upright again and looked at the mirror, a gorgon-like apparition appeared there. My tresses serpentined in all directions. I quite looked like a madwoman.

"Well, good," I grumbled, striding at an unladylike rate of speed out my door, down the back stairs, and out to the cab.

In it, I found Cecily but not Sherlock.

"The gentleman decided to walk home, Miss Enola," Harold informed me cheerfully enough—Sherlock must have paid him handsomely—but the news cheered me not at all. I felt a nearly childish pang, wanting him back, wanting him to come along with me to beard Sir Eustace.

I was attempting to remind myself that I would do

quite well on my own as Harold asked, "Where to next, Miss Enola?"

At that moment, Cecily saw my hair and came to life. "Enola!" She popped up from her seat. "What a glorious leonine mane! Have you been bicycling?"

I had to smile. "Hardly, when I have been with you all evening."

"Really? I don't remember. Where are we, and what are we doing here?"

"Alistairs'," I told Harold succinctly as I got into the cab; he knew the address. Then, as we rolled away, I turned back to Cecily. "Do you remember working at the telephone exchange?"

"Yes! I quite liked it, and I was good at it. But then you and your brother came, and—and the rest is a blank." As she said that, distress tightened her lovely face. "Enola, why can't I remember? There must be something wrong with me."

How I felt for her! But there was no time for sentiment, not when we had to face her father. I said, as stoutly as I could, "By recognizing it, you are well on your way to overcoming it."

"But what is it? What is happening to me?"

Maybe someday we would discuss it at length. But I said only, "You have misplaced perhaps an hour. It doesn't matter, so long as you can remain strong now and stand up to your father."

"Papa! If he knew the truth about me, he would lock me up in a lunatic asylum." Moaning, rocking, she hid her face in her hands.

"Truth? What truth? That you are left-handed? Cecily, please recall to mind the truth you know about *him,* and that with it, you could put him in *gaol.*"

I am sure I had never spoken to her so sternly ever before. Perhaps no one had, except her father, who roared and bullied. But despite my leonine mane, I was not roaring. Perhaps I was angry, but not at her.

Cecily became silent and still, then sat up straight and looked at me. I looked back. In the shadows of the cab, I could see very little except that her eyes shone with tears. She dried them with her handkerchief, dropped it on the seat of the cab, then offered me her hand. Her left hand, to my profound relief.

Then the cab slowed to a halt at the kerb in front of her house.

Chapter the Nineteenth

When the stone-faced butler, Smythe, opened the front door and saw me standing there arm in arm with Cecily, she in her workaday brown suit and I with unruly hair worthy of a barbarian, his facade cracked slightly. His mouth opened without changing shape, like a puppet's, and no speech issued forth.

"Hello, Smythe; are Mama and Papa home?" sang Cecily, breezing into the foyer with me by her side. She waved at the butler in passing—with her left hand, but I could feel my heart pounding in an extremity of hope and fear: hope that she could stand up to her father and fear that she might fail.

"Smythe, who's there?" bellowed a voice, unmistakably that of Sir Eustace, from the library. His inquiry seemed odd to me, given that he had just heard his daughter speak. But the next moment I realized he had never before heard such blithe tones from Cecily.

Yet Sir Eustace must have concluded or suspected something, because, without waiting for Smythe to answer, he came slamming out of the library, all five plump and jowly feet of him. Necessarily, because he stood in our way, Cecily and I halted. Her father's porcine eyes enlarged to a nearly normal size at the sight of us.

"You! Madwoman!" He pointed at me as if his finger were a dueling pistol, seemingly oblivious to his own daughter, who had been lost and now was found, standing beside me. "You, crazy thief! Where is my property that you stole? Return it at once or I shall send for a constable!"

I did not speak, must not speak, must allow Cecily this moment of destiny to be weak or strong—but everything seemed to stop, just stop. I did not breathe, could not move a finger even to clasp Cecily's hand, and never has silence drummed so loud in my ears or stretched—

"You shall do nothing of the sort, Father!" Cecily's voice rang out, martial, commanding. "It is I who should summon the police to put you in gaol for what you have done!"

He gawked at her, speechless, whether from sudden recognition or the shock of what she had said.

"You shall never lock me in my room again, Father," she said, more softly but somehow even more strongly.

Now I could speak. "We know who Timothy Burke was, and Imogen Saunders, and the misfortunate Sims, and what you did with their mortal remains and those of many more."

"We can prove it," said Cecily.

Now I could squeeze her hand in encouragement. "Yes, indeed. We have your most interesting record of the transactions. No doubt a search of public records—"

A wordless roar from Sir Eustace preempted anything more I had to say. Shoulders hunched, head thrust forwards as if he were a bull about to charge me, he shouted, "You, whoever you are, get out of here and never come near my daughter again!"

I felt Cecily start to tremble, and her hand went limp in my grasp. She slumped, hanging her head. Once more she had lost her true, left-handed self. I knew she could not help it, yet I felt like weeping with frustration.

Sir Eustace had not finished bellowing. "No one defies me. No one tells me what to do in my home! Out with you, or I'll lock you in the cellar!" He advanced upon me.

The fool intended to engage physically with me! I let go of Cecily's hand and reached for the dagger sheathed in the front of my corset.

But I did not draw it, for "Hush your nonsense, Alistair," sounded a voice, angelic and imperious, from above.

Sir Eustace jerked to a startled stop, and no wonder, if he thought his wife was still locked in her boudoir. I saw his piggy eyes pop open as he spun around to look behind him.

There, with her perfectly coifed head held high,

dressed to her utmost in an elegant emerald gown of three fabrics, her dignity unmarred by her two youngest children, a toddler and a five-year-old clinging to her skirt as if they would never again let her go—there stood Lady Theodora. Even as I stared, she came strolling down the main staircase arm in arm with Lady Vienna Steadwell.

Lady Vienna! I had all but forgotten about her. What was she doing, still here in this mansion of unpleasantness? I had expected she would take a cab home at her earliest opportunity.

How presumptuous of me. Evidently, Lady Vienna and Lady Theodora had become quite good friends in the course of the afternoon, which had obviously also included a reunion between Lady Theodora and her babies.

Having descended the stairs, Lady Theodora stood on the landing as if on a dais, with lifted chin. "I have already written the letters, Alistair," she told her husband, "and addressed them to the *Times*, the *Pall Mall Gazette*, the *Daily Telegraph*, and every other newspaper in London. If you do not wish to find yourself embroiled in a most shameful scandal, you will treat me and my daughter with much, much more respect from now on."

Cecily raised her head to look at her mother, then let go of me and ran, impetuous as a child, to Lady Theodora, flinging her arms around her and laying her head on her shoulder. Lady Theodora held her close, patting her and murmuring.

"Lady Theodora," I called across the room, "do you prefer scandal for him or gaol? Or both?"

Sir Eustace, to my satisfaction, seemed unable to speak. His face had congested and turned the colour of a plum, as if at any moment he might fall down in a fit of apoplexy. Conscience obliges me to admit I felt very scant concern for him.

Looking at me with a smile in answer to my question, Lady Theodora held her daughter and gave an expressive shrug. "It doesn't matter to me. I have been an obedient wife; I need not be ashamed of anything."

Sir Eustace began to emit sputtering noises reminiscent of the sound of grease dripping into a fire, as when a fat goose upon the turnspit is cooked.

Seizing the moment, I advanced upon him. I am,

unfortunately for a female, nearly as tall as my brother Sherlock, and, with my shocking hair, I am sure I looked like a raving Amazon. "You see, Sir Eustace, there are three of us who can destroy you."

"Four," said a serene voice, that of Lady Vienna Steadwell.

"Four of us," I amended, "all of whom possess photographic copies of your records—" Well, I must see to it that they would possess them in the very near future. "—to prove that you most unethically sold the bodies of deceased servants for personal gain, even going so far as shearing their hair for the wig trade or extracting their teeth to be made into dentures." I pulled out my list of conditions. "Therefore, listen, or else there shall be consequences. First and foremost, neither Lady Theodora, Lady Cecily, nor any of the latter's sisters are ever again to be confined to bedrooms—"

Languidly opening her formidable fan, Lady Vienna spoke up, her voice so sweet and placid that it overpowered any other. "I plan to invite Lady Cecily to come to Vienna with me."

Cecily raised her head from her mother's shoulder to look, her mouth an O. All of us gawked at Lady

Vienna in much the same way, except Lady Theodora, who smiled rather like the Mona Lisa.

Lady Vienna gestured airily with ivory, point lace, garnets, and crocodile skin. "Theodora and I were talking. You know, I have always wanted to visit the city after which I am named, and by accompanying me, Cecily could avail herself of the services of certain doctors there, physicians who are specializing in a new school of medicine."

"Marvelous!" I exclaimed, beaming my thanks at Lady Vienna.

At the same moment, Sir Eustace squawked, "What? Balderdash! I will not have—"

I turned on him. "You will not have *anything* except a scandal and possibly a gaol sentence, Sir Eustace, if you do not change your ways."

He turned his red, contorted face my way. "You! Meddling in my affairs! Who the blasted blazes do you think you are?"

It would have been most unwise of me to tell him my name.

"The one who is going to stop you from being a sneak thief and a bully," I said.

"As I told you before, she is my niece Aubergina," said Lady Vienna.

"She is my courageous and most greatly esteemed sister," said a quite aristocratic and commanding male voice.

"Sherlock!" I gasped, turning. There, inside the front door (which the sorely perturbed butler had never properly closed), towered my brother, top hat and all.

"Dear boy!" cried Lady Vienna to him. "I have not seen you since you were in short pants!"

"Aunt Vienna." Doffing his hat, he bowed to her. "I'm flattered that you remember me. If my sister has concluded her business here, would you care to share a cab with us?"

"My dear Aubergina, have you concluded your business?" asked Lady Vienna.

My brother's straight mouth twitched in amusement at my pseudonym. Careful not to smile back, I turned to face once more the belligerent baronet.

"Sir Eustace, do you agree to the conditions?" I demanded, considering that it did not matter whether I had read them off to him. Ultimately, they were all one: he could rule the household like a tyrant no more.

"Do I have a choice?" Now he sounded sulky.

"Not at all. Agree or Lady Theodora mails her letters. In fact, I will take them and post them for her straightaway."

Sir Eustace gave forth a wordless blatancy.

I insisted. "Sir Eustace, do you agree to mend your ways? Yes or no."

"Yes," he growled, then turned towards the back of the house and stormed out of sight.

"Whatever are you doing here?" I asked Sherlock as we climbed into the cab—just the two of us, for Lady Vienna had been most pleased to stay on as a houseguest (and reinforcement, I am sure) at Lady Theodora's request. "Harold said you were walking home."

"Your friend Harold is a paragon among cabbies. He very kindly allowed me to hide under his seat."

"But why? I thought you had no wish to besmirch your hands with this sordid business."

"But I quite wished to watch the fireworks. Why on earth did you go with your hair looking such a fright?"

"Exactly. Fright."

"Ah."

For a while, I remained silent, enjoying pleasant thoughts as the cab jounced us along: Had Sherlock really wanted nothing more than to enjoy the fireworks? Or had he truly wished to keep his distance but brotherly concern had driven him to come along with me?

Hidden in the shadows of the cab, I let myself smile, but I would never ask him that question.

"Enola." Evidently, Sherlock had some thoughts of his own. "Now that the dust of battle is settling, would you mind telling me: How did you know where to find Lady Cecily? Had she somehow communicated her intentions to you without my knowledge?"

Still smiling, I shook my head.

"Enunciate, please."

"No, she sent me no more messages. But finding her was simplicity itself, my dear Sherlock." I mimicked his sometimes pedantic tone. "I reasoned it out by the process of elimination. Cecily had to seek gainful employment, but she is too much of a lady to work in a factory, and as for office or newspaper work, she does not know how to use a typewriter. To clerk in a shop or even in a post office, she would require more presentable clothing, likewise to be a nanny or governess. Thus, very few possibilities remained. Moreover, from previous conversation, I knew her to be quite interested in telephones. Hence, I felt reasonably sure of finding her in a telephone exchange."

If Dr. Watson had been there, he might have cried, "Wonderful!" I would have liked some effusions of that sort, but Sherlock merely said, "I see," in a dubious tone. "But why that particular exchange? There are several."

"Because Cecily knows the East End from previous sorties and misadventures. People under duress tend to return to areas they know."

"Ah," said Sherlock.

After that, there was again silence until the cab drew up in front of the Professional Women's Club. As Harold waited patiently, holding Brownie's reins, my brother spoke, and not just to bid me good night.

"Enola, what are your plans?" he asked rather abruptly.

"Arrange with Harold to let me hide some peculiar items in his stable. Sleep, then tomorrow do something to tame my hair. Return to my sorely neglected studies."

"Other than that, I am sure the academy can spare

you a few more days. Have you any matters of urgency in hand?"

"None." I thought of hinting that I, like him, enjoyed musical performances, then sighed due to a sense of futility. "But I am sure you do."

"As a matter of fact, a most peculiar case has come my way, and I was thinking that you, with your uniquely intelligent feminine perspective . . . Could you perhaps see your way clear to consulting with me upon the matter?"

First, I said in a calm, ladylike way, "Of course, my dear brother." Then I gave a sort of hoot, turned, and flung my arms around his neck.

"My dear Enola!" He sounded startled but not unpleased, and he disengaged himself from me quite gently. "Tomorrow, then, for luncheon? Baker Street?"

"I shall wear my very best hat."

"Heavens have mercy."

He helped me out, and I stood on the pavement laughing and waving as the cab rolled away.

Epilogue

Boarding the steamship that would ferry her and Lady Vienna across the English Channel, Cecily felt she had seldom seen anything as beautiful as the sleek vessel with two tall smokestacks and even taller flagpoles with colours flying high, like her spirits. She had triumphed over her father's schemes and defied his despotism, and she was getting away from him, going to the Continent!

Thanks to a near-miracle in the form of Lady Vienna Steadwell, the only adult Cecily had ever met who really comprehended her plight—because Lady Vienna had been born left-handed, too, and seemed to fully understood what Cecily was going through. And supported her in her struggle. And, moreover, showed signs of liking her! Cecily liked Lady Vienna tremendously.

Once on deck, she and Lady Vienna stood side by side at the rail. Looking down on the brightly dressed well-wishers left behind on the dock, Cecily could feel the sea breeze stirring her flaxen hair—which remained quite short, like that of an orphan, but Cecily did not at the moment care whether people looked askance at her. The fresh air, with its brisk salt tang, matched her inner sense of making a fresh start.

Hands on the ship's railing, she smiled down at her mother and the one other person who had come to see her off: Enola, wearing the latest fashion, looking stylish yet raffish as only Enola could do, with a veritable orchard of cherries springing from her hat brim to match her cherry-red polonaise. Enola's smile glinted with a hint of mischief. Yet it seemed to Cecily that, even standing next to Mum, Enola seemed rather lonely. Her friends, after all, were sailing away.

Cecily wondered when she would see Enola again

and how she would do without her. The channel crossing, often rough, might make her seasick. People in France might mock her efforts to speak their language. . . .

As if a drain had opened, all confidence and happiness flowed away, and her selfhood whirlpooled down, down, down until she felt like a timid, naive, nearly helpless creature terrified to venture so far from home—

No.

She had felt this way before, but this time was different because she had started to understand what was happening, and—

"Cecily, are you all right?" Lady Vienna asked.

"I will be," Cecily whispered.

At that moment, the ship's horn blared so that no one could possibly hear her. They were casting off. Slowly, slowly, the deck began in a terrifying way to move beneath Cecily's feet. She clutched hard at the railing with both hands.

Lady Vienna turned to look at her. "Cecily?"

Cecily did not look back. Her gaze was fixed on the dock below, where, across an ever-widening distance, Enola was waving, waving goodbye.

Cecily sensed what she had to do, and, for her friend's sake, she mustered the grit to do it. She made herself let go of the ship's rail. And she lifted her hand high. And she waved at Enola.

Her left hand.